This Book Belongs to
Tony and Nicole

Alice in Wonderland

By

LEWIS CARROLL

Illustrated by

MARJORIE TORREY

Abridged and prepared under the supervision of JOSETTE FRANK,
Children's Book Adviser of the Child Study Association of America

RANDOM HOUSE · NEW YORK

1 Down the Rabbit-Hole

Alice was beginning to get very tired of sitting by her sister on the bank and of having nothing to do: once or twice she had peeped into the book her sister was reading, but it had no pictures or conversations in it, "and what is the use of a book," thought Alice, "without pictures or conversations?"

So she was considering, in her own mind (as well as she could, for the hot day made her feel very sleepy and stupid), whether the pleasure of making a daisy-chain would be worth the trouble of getting up and picking the daisies, when suddenly a White Rabbit with pink eyes ran close by her.

There was nothing so *very* remarkable in that; nor did Alice think it so *very* much out of the way to hear the Rabbit say to itself "Oh dear! Oh dear! I shall be too late!" but, when the Rabbit actually *took a watch out of its waistcoat-pocket,* and looked at it, and then hurried on, Alice started to her feet, and burning with curiosity, she ran across the field after it, and was just in time to see it pop down a large rabbit-hole under the hedge.

In another moment down went Alice after it, never once considering how in the world she was to get out again.

The rabbit-hole went straight on like a tunnel for some way, and then dipped suddenly down, so suddenly that Alice had not a moment to think about stopping herself before she found herself falling down what seemed to be a very deep well.

Either the well was very deep, or she fell very slowly, for she had plenty of time as she went down to look about her, and to wonder what was going to happen next. First, she tried to look down and make out what she was coming to, but it was too dark to see anything: then she looked at the sides of the well, and noticed that they were filled with cupboards and book-shelves: here and there she saw maps and pictures hung upon pegs. She took down a jar from one of the shelves; it was labeled Orange Marmalade.

Down, down, down. Would the fall *never* come to an end? "I wonder how many miles I've fallen by this time?" she said aloud. "I must be getting somewhere near the center of the earth. Let me see: that would be four thousand miles down, I think—yes, that's about the right distance —but then I wonder what Latitude or Longitude I've got to?" (Alice had not the slightest idea what Latitude was, or Longitude either, but she thought they were nice grand words to say.)

Presently she began again. "I wonder if I shall fall right *through* the earth! How funny it'll seem to come out among the people that walk with their heads downwards!"

Down, down, down. There was nothing else to do, so Alice soon began talking again. "Dinah'll miss me very much tonight, I should think!" (Dinah was the cat.) "I hope they'll remember her saucer of milk at tea-time." Here Alice began to get rather sleepy, and had just begun to dream that she was walking hand in hand with Dinah when suddenly, thump! thump! down she came upon a heap of sticks and dry leaves, and the fall was over.

Alice was not a bit hurt, and she jumped up on to her feet in a moment: she looked up, but it was all dark overhead: before her was another long passage,

and the White Rabbit was still in sight, hurrying down it. There was not a moment to be lost: away went Alice like the wind, and was just in time to hear it say, as it turned a corner, "Oh my ears and whiskers, how late it's getting!" She was close behind it when she turned the corner, but the Rabbit was no longer to be seen: she found herself in a long, low hall, which was lit up by a row of lamps hanging from the roof.

There were doors all round the hall, but they were all locked; and when Alice had been all the way down one side and up the other, trying every door, she walked sadly down the middle, wondering how she was ever to get out again.

Suddenly she came upon a little three-legged table, all made of solid glass. There was nothing on it but a tiny golden key, and Alice's first idea was that this might belong to one of the doors of the hall; but, alas! either the locks were too large, or the key was too small, but at any rate it would not open any of them. However, on the second time round, she came upon a low curtain she had not noticed before, and behind it was a little door about fifteen inches high: she tried the little golden key in the lock, and to her great delight it fitted!

Alice opened the door and found that it led into a small passage, not much larger than a rat-hole: she knelt down and looked along the passage into the loveliest garden you ever saw. How she longed to get out of that dark hall, and wander about among those beds of bright flowers and those cool fountains, but she could not even get her head through the doorway; "and even if my head *would* go through," thought poor Alice, "it would be of very little use without my shoulders. Oh, how I wish I could shut up like a telescope! I think I could, if I only knew how to begin."

There seemed to be no use in waiting by the little door, so she went back to the table, half hoping she might find another key on it, or at any rate a book of rules for shutting people up like telescopes: this time she found a little bottle on it ("which certainly was not here before," said Alice), and tied round the neck of the bottle was a paper label, with the words "DRINK ME" beautifully printed on it in large letters.

It was all very well to say "Drink me," but the wise little Alice was not going to do *that* in a hurry. "No, I'll look first," she said, "and see whether it's marked '*poison*' or not."

However, this bottle was *not* marked "poison," so Alice ventured to taste it, and, finding it very nice (it had, in fact, a sort of mixed flavor of cherry-tart, custard, pine-apple, roast turkey, toffy, and hot buttered toast), she very soon finished it off.

"What a curious feeling!" said Alice. "I must be shutting up like a telescope!"

And so it was indeed: she was now only ten inches high, and her face brightened up at the thought that she was now the right size for going through the little door into that lovely garden. First, however, she waited for a few minutes to see if she was going to shrink any further.

After a while, finding that nothing more happened, she decided on going into the garden at once; but, alas for poor Alice! when she got to the door, she found she had forgotten the little golden key, and when she went back to the table for it, she found she could not possibly reach it: she could see it quite plainly through the glass, and she tried her best to climb up one of the legs of the table, but it was too slippery; and when she had tired herself out with trying, the poor little thing sat down and cried.

"Come, there's no use in crying like that!" said Alice to herself rather sharply. "I advise you to leave off this minute!" She generally gave herself very good advice (though she very seldom followed it).

Soon her eye fell on a little glass box that was lying under the table: she opened it, and found in it a very small cake, on which the words "EAT ME" were beautifully marked in currants. "Well, I'll eat it," said Alice "and if it makes me grow larger, I can reach the key; and if it makes me grow smaller, I can creep under the door: so either way I'll get into the garden, and I don't care which happens!"

She ate a little bit, and said anxiously to herself "Which way? Which way?", holding her hand on the top of her head to feel which way it was growing; and she was quite surprised to find that she remained the same size.

So she set to work, and very soon finished off the cake.

2 The Pool of Tears

"Curiouser and curiouser!" cried Alice (she was so much surprised, that for the moment she quite forgot how to speak good English). "Now I'm opening out like the largest telescope that ever was! Good-bye, feet!" (for when she looked down at her feet, they seemed to be almost out of sight, they were getting so far off).

Just at this moment her head struck against the roof of the hall: in fact she was now rather more than nine feet high, and she at once took up the little golden key and hurried off to the garden door.

Poor Alice! It was as much as she could do, lying down on one side, to look through into the garden with one eye; but to get through was more hopeless than ever: she sat down and began to cry again.

"You ought to be ashamed of yourself," said Alice, "a great girl like you to go on crying in this way! Stop this moment, I tell you!" But she went on all the same, shedding gallons of tears, until there was a large pool all round her, about four inches deep and reaching half down the hall.

After a time she heard a little pattering of feet in the distance, and she hastily dried her eyes to see what was coming. It was the White Rabbit returning, splendidly dressed, with a pair of white kid-gloves in one hand and a large fan in the other: he came trotting along in a great hurry, muttering to himself, as he came, "Oh! The Duchess, the Duchess! Oh! *Won't* she be savage if I've kept her waiting!" Alice felt so desperate that she was ready to ask help of any one: so, when the Rabbit came near her, she began, in a low, timid voice, "If you please, Sir——" The Rabbit started violently, dropped the white kid-gloves and the fan, and scurried away into the darkness as hard as he could go.

Alice took up the fan and gloves, and, as the hall was very hot, she kept fanning herself all the time she went on talking. "Dear, dear! How queer everything is to-day! And yesterday things went on just as usual. I wonder if I've changed in the night? I'll try if I know all the things I used to know. Let me see: four times five is twelve, and four times six is thirteen, and four times seven is —oh dear! I shall never get to twenty at that rate! I'll try and say *'How doth the little—',*" and she crossed her hands on her lap, as if she were saying lessons, and began to repeat it, but her voice sounded hoarse and strange, and the words did not come the same as they used to do:

"How doth the little crocodile
Improve his shining tail,
And pour the waters of the Nile
On every golden scale!

"How cheerfully he seems to grin,
How neatly spreads his claws,
And welcomes little fishes in,
With gently smiling jaws!

"I'm sure those are not the right words," said poor Alice, and her eyes filled with tears again. "Oh dear! I am so *very* tired of being all alone here!"

As she said this she looked down at her hands, and was surprised to see that she had put on one of the Rabbit's little white kid-gloves while she was talking. "How *can* I have done that?" she thought. "I must be growing small again." She got up and went to the table to measure herself by it, and found that, as nearly as she could guess, she was now about two feet high, and was going on shrinking rapidly: she soon found out that the cause of this was the fan she was holding, and she dropped it hastily, just in time to save herself from shrinking away altogether.

"That *was* a narrow escape!" said Alice, a good deal frightened at the sudden change, but very glad to find herself still in existence. "And now for the garden!" And she ran with all speed back to the little door; but, alas! the little door was shut again, and the little golden key was lying on the glass table as before, "and things are worse than ever," thought the poor child, "for I never was so small as this before, never! And I declare it's too bad, that it is!"

As she said these words her foot slipped, and in another moment, splash! she was up to her chin in salt-water. Her first idea was that she had somehow fallen into the sea. However, she soon made out that she was in the pool of tears which she had wept when she was nine feet high.

"I wish I hadn't cried so much!" said Alice, as she swam about, trying to find her way out. "I shall be punished for it now, I suppose, by being drowned in my own tears! That *will* be a queer thing, to be sure! However, everything is queer to-day."

Just then she heard something splashing about in the pool a little way off, and she swam nearer to make out what it was: at first she thought it must be a walrus or hippopotamus, but then she remembered how small she was now, and she soon made out that it was only a mouse, that had slipped in like herself.

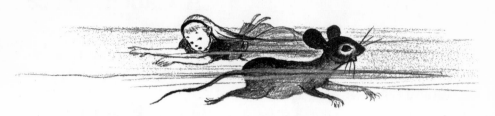

"Would it be of any use, now," thought Alice, "to speak to this mouse? Everything is so out-of-the-way down here, that I should think very likely it can talk: at any rate, there's no harm in trying." So she began: "O Mouse, do you know the way out of this pool? I am very tired of swimming about here, O Mouse!"

The mouse looked at her rather inquisitively, and seemed to her to wink with one of its little eyes, but it said nothing.

"Perhaps it doesn't understand English," thought Alice. "I daresay it's a French mouse. So she began again: "Où est ma chatte?" which was the first sentence in her French lesson-book. The Mouse gave a sudden leap out of the water, and seemed to quiver all over with fright. "Oh, I beg your pardon!" cried Alice hastily, afraid that she had hurt the poor animal's feelings. "I quite forgot you didn't like cats."

"Our family always *hated* cats: nasty, low, vulgar things!" cried the Mouse, who was trembling down to the end of its tail. "Don't let me hear the name again!"

"I won't indeed!" said Alice, in a great hurry to change the subject of conversation. "Are you—are you fond—of—of dogs!" The Mouse did not answer, so Alice went on eagerly: "There is such a nice little dog, near our house, I should like to show you! A little bright-eyed terrier, you know, with oh, such long curly brown hair! It belongs to a farmer, you know, and he says it's so useful. He says it kills all the rats and—oh dear!" cried Alice in a sorrowful tone. "I'm afraid I've offended it again!" For the Mouse was swimming away from her as hard as it could go, and making quite a commotion in the pool as it went.

So she called softly after it, "Mouse dear! Do come back again, and we won't talk about cats, or dogs either, if you don't like them!" When the Mouse heard this, it turned round and swam slowly back to her: its face was quite pale and it said, in a low trembling voice, "Let us get to the shore."

It was high time to go, for the pool was getting quite crowded with the birds and animals that had fallen into it: there was a Duck and a Dodo, a Lory and an Eaglet, and several other curious creatures. Alice led the way, and the whole party swam to the shore.

3   A Caucus-Race

They were indeed a queer-looking party that assembled on the bank—the birds with draggled feathers, the animals with their fur clinging close to them, and all dripping wet, cross, and uncomfortable.

The first question of course was, how to get dry again: they had a consultation about this, and after a few minutes it seemed quite natural to Alice to find herself talking familiarly with them, as if she had known them all her life. The best thing to get us dry would be a Caucus-race," said the Dodo.

"What *is* a Caucus-race?" said Alice.

"Why," said the Dodo, "the best way to explain it is to do it."

First it marked out a race-course, in a sort of circle, ("the exact shape doesn't matter," it said,) and then all the party were placed along the course, here and there. There was no "One, two, three, and away!" but they began running when they liked, and left off when they liked, so that it was not easy to know when the race was over. However, when they had been running half an hour or so, and were quite dry again, the Dodo suddenly called out "The race is over!" and they all crowded round it, panting, and asking, "But who has won?"

This question the Dodo could not answer without a great deal of thought, and it stood for a long time with one finger pressed upon its forehead while the rest waited in silence. At last the Dodo said *"Everybody* has won, and *all* must have prizes."

"But who is to give the prizes?" quite a chorus of voices asked.

"Why, *she,* of course," said the Dodo, pointing to Alice with one finger; and the whole party at once crowded round her, calling out, in a confused way, "Prizes! Prizes!"

Alice had no idea what to do, and in despair she put her hand in her pocket, and pulled out a box of comfits (luckily the salt-water had not got into it), and handed them round as prizes. There was exactly one a-piece, all round.

"But she must have a prize herself, you know," said the Mouse.

"Of course," the Dodo replied very gravely. "What else have you got in your pocket?" it went on, turning to Alice.

"Only a thimble," said Alice sadly.

"Hand it over here," said the Dodo.

Then they all crowded round her once more, while the Dodo solemnly presented the thimble, saying "We beg your acceptance of this elegant thimble"; and, when it had finished this short speech, they all cheered.

Alice thought the whole thing very absurd, but they all looked so grave that she did not dare to laugh; and, as she could not think of anything to say, she simply bowed, and took the thimble, looking as solemn as she could.

"I wish I had our Dinah here!" said Alice aloud, addressing nobody in particular.

"And who is Dinah, if I might venture to ask the question?" said the Lory.

Alice replied eagerly, for she was always ready to talk about her pet: "Dinah's our cat. And she's such a capital one for catching mice, you can't think! And oh, I wish you could see her after the birds! Why, she'll eat a little bird as soon as look at it!"

This speech caused a remarkable sensation among the party. Some of the birds hurried off at once: one old Magpie began wrapping itself up very carefully, remarking "I really must be getting home: the night-air doesn't suit my throat!" And a Canary called out in a trembling voice, to its children, "Come away, my dears! It's high time you were all in bed!" On various pretexts they all moved off, and Alice was soon left alone.

"I wish I hadn't mentioned Dinah!" she said to herself in a melancholy tone. "Nobody seems to like her, down here, and I'm sure she's the best cat in the world! Oh, my dear Dinah! I wonder if I shall ever see you any more!" And here poor Alice began to cry again, for she felt very lonely and low-spirited.

 In a little while, however, she again heard a little pattering of footsteps in the distance, and she looked up eagerly.

4 The White Rabbit's House

It was the White Rabbit, trotting slowly back again, and looking anxiously about as it went, as if it had lost something; and she heard it muttering to itself, "The Duchess! The Duchess! Oh my dear paws! Oh my fur and whiskers! She'll get me executed, as sure as ferrets are ferrets! Where *can* I have dropped them, I wonder?" Alice guessed in a moment that it was looking for the fan and the pair of white kid-gloves, and she very good-naturedly began hunting about for them, but they were nowhere to be seen—everything seemed to have changed since her swim in the pool; and the great hall, with the glass table and the little door, had vanished completely.

Very soon the Rabbit noticed Alice, as she went hunting about, and called out to her, in an angry tone, "Why, Mary Ann, what *are* you doing out here? Run home this moment, and fetch me a pair of gloves and a fan! Quick, now!" And Alice was so much frightened that she ran off at once in the direction it pointed to, without trying to explain the mistake that it had made.

"He took me for his housemaid," she said to herself as she ran. "How surprised he'll be when he finds out who I am! But I'd better take him his fan and gloves—that is, if I can find them." As she said this, she came upon a neat little house, on the door of which was a bright brass plate with the name "W. RABBIT" engraved upon it. She went in without knocking, and hurried upstairs, in great fear lest she should meet the real Mary Ann, and be turned out of the house before she had found the fan and gloves.

"How queer it seems," Alice said to herself, "to be going messages for a rabbit! I suppose Dinah'll be sending me on messages next!"

By this time she had found her way into a tidy little room with a table in the window, and on it (as she had hoped) a fan and two or three pairs of tiny white kid-gloves: she took up the fan and a pair of the gloves, and was just going to leave the room, when her eye fell upon a little bottle that stood near the looking-glass. There was no label this time with the words "DRINK ME," but nevertheless she uncorked it and put it to her lips. "I know *something* interesting is sure to happen," she said to herself, "whenever I eat or drink anything: so I'll just see what this bottle does. I do hope it'll make me grow large again, for really I'm quite tired of being such a tiny little thing!"

It did so indeed, and much sooner than she had expected: before she had drunk half the bottle, she found her head pressing against the ceiling, and had to stoop to save her neck from being broken. She hastily put down the bottle, saying to herself "That's quite enough—I hope I shan't grow any more—As it is, I can't get out at the door—I do wish I hadn't drunk quite so much!"

Alas! It was too late to wish that! She went on growing, and growing, and very soon had to kneel down on the floor: in another minute there was not even room for this, and she tried the effect of lying down with one elbow against

the door, and the other arm curled round her head. Still she went on growing, and, as a last resource, she put one arm out of the window, and one foot up the chimney, and said to herself "Now I can do no more, whatever happens. What *will* become of me?"

Luckily for Alice, the little magic bottle had now had its full effect, and she grew no larger: still it was very uncomfortable, and, as there seemed to be no sort of chance of her ever getting out of the room again, no wonder she felt unhappy.

"It was much pleasanter at home," thought poor Alice, "when one wasn't always growing larger and smaller, and being ordered about by mice and rabbits. I almost wish I hadn't gone down that rabbit-hole—and yet—and yet—it's rather curious, you know, this sort of life! I do wonder what *can* have happened to me! When I used to read fairy tales, I fancied that kind of thing never happened, and now here I am in the middle of one! There ought to be a book written about me, that there ought! And when I grow up, I'll write one—but I'm grown up now," she added in a sorrowful tone: "at least there's no room to grow up any more *here*."

After a few minutes she heard a voice outside.

"Mary Ann! Mary Ann!" said the voice. "Fetch me my gloves this moment!" Then came a little pattering of feet on the stairs. Alice knew it was the Rabbit coming to look for her, and she trembled till she shook the house, quite forgetting that she was now about a thousand times as large as the Rabbit, and had no reason to be afraid of it.

Presently the Rabbit came up to the door, and tried to open it; but, as the door opened inwards, and Alice's elbow was pressed hard against it, that attempt proved a failure. Alice heard it say to itself "Then I'll go round and get in at the window."

"*That* you won't!" thought Alice, and, after waiting till she fancied she heard the Rabbit just under the window, she suddenly spread out her hand, and made a snatch in the air. She did not get hold of anything, but she heard a little shriek and a fall, and a crash of broken glass, from which she concluded that it was just possible it had fallen into a cucumber-frame, or something of the sort.

Next came an angry voice—the Rabbit's—"Pat! Pat! Where are you?" And then a voice she had never heard before, "Sure then I'm here! Digging for apples, yer honor!"

"Digging for apples, indeed!" said the Rabbit angrily. "Here! Come and help me out of *this*!" (Sounds of more broken glass.)

"Now tell me, Pat, what's that in the window?"

"Sure, it's an arm, yer honor!"

"An arm, you goose! Who ever saw one that size? Why, it fills the whole window!"

"Sure, it does, yer honor: but it's an arm for all that."

"Well, it's got no business there, at any rate: go and take it away!"

There was a long silence after this, and Alice could only hear whispers now and then; such as "Sure, I don't like it, yer honor, at all, at all!" "Do as I tell you, you coward!" and at last she spread out her hand again, and made another snatch in the air. This time there were *two* little shrieks, and more sounds of broken glass. "I wonder what they'll do next!" thought Alice. "As for pulling me out of the window, I only wish *they could*! I'm sure *I* don't want to stay in here any longer! If they had any sense, they'd take the roof off."

After a minute or two they began moving about again, and Alice heard the Rabbit say "A barrowful will do, to begin with."

"A barrowful of *what?*" thought Alice. But she had not long to doubt, for the next moment a shower of little pebbles came rattling in at the window, and

some of them hit her in the face. "I'll put a stop to this," she said to herself, and shouted out "You'd better not do that again!" which produced another dead silence.

Alice noticed, with some surprise, that the pebbles were all turning into little cakes as they lay on the floor, and a bright idea came into her head. "If I eat one of these cakes," she thought, "it's sure to make *some* change in my size; and, as it can't possibly make me larger, it must make me smaller, I suppose."

So she swallowed one of the cakes, and was delighted to find that she began shrinking directly. As soon as she was small enough to get through the door, she ran out of the house, and found quite a crowd of little animals and birds waiting outside. They all made a rush at Alice the moment she appeared; but she ran off as hard as she could, and soon found herself safe in a thick wood.

"The first thing I've got to do," said Alice to herself, as she wandered about in the wood, "is to grow to my right size again; and the second thing is to find my way into that lovely garden. I think that will be the best plan."

It sounded an excellent plan, no doubt, and very neatly and simply arranged: the only difficulty was, that she had not the smallest idea how to set about it. "I suppose I ought to eat or drink something or other," she said; "but the great question is 'What?'"

The great question certainly was "What?" Alice looked all round her at the flowers and the blades of grass, but she could not see anything that looked like the right thing to eat or drink under the circumstances. There was a large mushroom growing near her, about the same height as herself; and, when she had looked under it, and on both sides of it, and behind it, it occurred to her that she might as well look and see what was on the top of it.

She stretched herself up on tiptoe, and peeped over the edge of the mushroom, and her eyes immediately met those of a large blue caterpillar, that was sitting on the top, with its arms folded, quietly smoking a long hookah, and taking not the smallest notice of her or of anything else.

5 Advice from a Caterpillar

The Caterpillar and Alice looked at each other for some time in silence: at last the Caterpillar took the hookah out of its mouth, and addressed her in a languid, sleepy voice.

"Who are *you?*" said the Caterpillar.

This was not an encouraging opening for a conversation. Alice replied, rather shyly, "I—I hardly know, Sir, just at present—at least I know who I *was* when I got up this morning, but I think I must have been changed several times since then."

"What do you mean by that?" said the Caterpillar, sternly. "Explain yourself!"

"I can't explain *myself,* I'm afraid, Sir," said Alice, "because I'm not myself, you see."

"I don't see," said the Caterpillar.

"I'm afraid I can't put it more clearly," Alice replied, very politely, "for I can't understand it myself, to begin with; and being so many different sizes in a day is very confusing."

"It isn't," said the Caterpillar.

Alice felt a little irritated at the Caterpillar's making such *very* short remarks, and she drew herself up and said, very gravely, "I think you ought to tell me who *you* are, first."

"Why?" said the Caterpillar.

Here was another puzzling question; and, as Alice could not think of any good reason, and the Caterpillar seemed to be in a *very* unpleasant state of mind, she turned away.

"Come back!" the Caterpillar called after her, "I've something important to say!"

This sounded promising, certainly. Alice turned and came back again.

"Keep your temper," said the Caterpillar.

"Is that all?" said Alice, swallowing down her anger as well as she could.

"No," said the Caterpillar. "What size do you want to be?" it asked.

"Well, I should like to be a *little* larger, Sir, if you wouldn't mind," said Alice: "three inches is such a wretched height to be."

"It is a very good height indeed!" said the Caterpillar angrily, rearing itself upright as it spoke (it was exactly three inches high).

"But I'm not used to it!" pleaded poor Alice in a piteous tone. And she thought to herself "I wish the creatures wouldn't be so easily offended!"

"You'll get used to it in time," said the Caterpillar; and it put the hookah into its mouth, and began smoking again.

This time Alice waited patiently until it chose to speak again. In a minute or two the Caterpillar took the hookah out of its mouth, and yawned once or twice, and shook itself. Then it got down off the mushroom, and crawled away into the grass, merely remarking, as it went, "One side will make you grow taller, and the other side will make you grow shorter."

"One side of *what?* The other side of *what?*" thought Alice to herself.

"Of the mushroom," said the Caterpillar, just as if she had asked it aloud; and in another moment it was out of sight.

Alice remained looking thoughtfully at the mushroom for a minute, trying to make out which were the two sides of it; and, as it was perfectly round, she found this a very difficult question. However, at last she stretched her arms round it as far as they would go, and broke off a bit of the edge with each hand.

"And now which is which?" she said to herself, and nibbled a little of the right-hand bit to try the effect. The next moment she felt a violent blow underneath her chin: it had struck her foot!

She was a good deal frightened by this very sudden change, but she felt that there was no time to be lost, as she was shrinking rapidly: so she set to work at once nibbling first at one piece and then at the other, and growing sometimes taller, and sometimes shorter, until she had succeeded in bringing herself to her usual height.

It was so long since she had been anything near the right size, that it felt quite strange at first; but she got used to it in a few minutes, and began talking to herself as usual, "Come, there's half my plan done now! The next thing is, to get into that beautiful garden—how *is* that to be done, I wonder?" As she said this, she came suddenly upon an open place, with a little house in it about four feet high. "Whoever lives there," thought Alice, "it'll never do to come upon them *this* size: why, I should frighten them out of their wits!" So she began nibbling at the right-hand bit again, and did not venture to go near the house till she had brought herself down to nine inches high.

For a minute or two she stood looking at the house, and wondering what to do next, when suddenly a footman in livery came running out of the wood— (she considered him to be a footman because he was in livery: otherwise, judging by his face only, she would have called him a fish)—and rapped loudly at the door with his knuckles. It was opened by another footman in livery, with a round face, and large eyes like a frog; and both footmen, Alice noticed, had powdered hair that curled all over their heads. She felt very curious to know what it was all about, and crept a little way out of the wood to listen.

The Fish-Footman began by producing from under his arm a great letter, nearly as large as himself, and this he handed over to the other, saying, in a solemn tone, "For the Duchess. An invitation from the Queen to play croquet." The Frog-Footman repeated, in the same solemn tone, only changing the order of the words a little, "From the Queen. An invitation for the Duchess to play croquet."

Then they both bowed low, and their curls got entangled together.

Alice laughed so much at this, that she had to run back into the wood for fear of their hearing her; and, when she next peeped out, the Fish-Footman

was gone, and the other was sitting on the ground near the door, staring stupidly up into the sky.

Alice went timidly up to the door, and knocked.

"There's no sort of use in knocking," said the Footman, "and that for two reasons. First, because I'm on the same side of the door as you are: secondly, because they're making such a noise inside, no one could possibly hear you." And certainly there *was* a most extraordinary noise going on within—a constant howling and sneezing, and every now and then a great crash, as if a dish or kettle had been broken to pieces.

"Please, then," said Alice, "how am I to get in?"

"*Are* you to get in at all?" said the Footman. "That's the first question, you know."

It was, no doubt: only Alice did not like to be told so. "It's really dreadful," she muttered to herself, "the way all the creatures argue. It's enough to drive one crazy! There's no use in talking to him," said Alice desperately: "he's perfectly idiotic!" And she opened the door and went in.

The door led right into a large kitchen, which was full of smoke from one end to the other: the Duchess was sitting on a three-legged stool in the middle, nursing a baby: the cook was leaning over the fire, stirring a large cauldron which seemed to be full of soup.

"There's certainly too much pepper in that soup!" Alice said to herself, as well as she could for sneezing.

There was certainly too much of it in the *air*. Even the Duchess sneezed occasionally; and as for the baby, it was sneezing and howling alternately without a moment's pause. The only two creatures in the kitchen, that did *not* sneeze, were the cook, and a large cat, which was lying on the hearth and grinning from ear to ear.

"Please would you tell me," said Alice, a little timidly, for she was not quite sure whether it was good manners for her to speak first, "why your cat grins like that?"

"It's a Cheshire-Cat," said the Duchess, "and that's why."

"I didn't know that Cheshire-Cats always grinned; in fact, I didn't know that cats *could* grin."

"They all can," said the Duchess; "and most of 'em do."

"I don't know of any that do," Alice said very politely, feeling quite pleased to have got into a conversation.

"You don't know much," said the Duchess; "and that's a fact."

Alice did not at all like the tone of this remark, and thought it would be as well to introduce some other subject of conversation. While she was trying to fix on one, the cook took the cauldron of soup off the fire, and at once set to work throwing everything within her reach at the Duchess and the baby— the fire-irons came first; then followed a shower of sauce-pans, plates, and dishes. The Duchess took no notice of them even when they hit her; and the baby was howling so much already, that it was quite impossible to say whether the blows hurt it or not.

"Oh, *please* mind what you're doing!" cried Alice, jumping up and down in an agony of terror. "Oh, there goes his *precious* nose!" as an unusually large sauce-pan flew close by it, and very nearly carried it off.

"If everybody minded their own business," the Duchess said, in a hoarse growl, "the world would go round a deal faster than it does.'"

And with that she began nursing her child again, singing a sort of lullaby to it as she did so, and giving it a violent shake at the end of every line:

"Speak roughly to your little boy,
And beat him when he sneezes:
He only does it to annoy,
Because he knows it teases."

CHORUS (in which the cook and the baby joined):
"Wow! wow! wow!"

While the Duchess sang the second verse of the song, she kept tossing the baby violently up and down, and the poor little thing howled so, that Alice could hardly hear the words:—

"I speak severely to my boy,
I beat him when he sneezes;
For he can thoroughly enjoy
The pepper when he pleases!"

CHORUS
"Wow! wow! wow!"

"Here! You may nurse it a bit, if you like!" the Duchess said to Alice, flinging the baby at her as she spoke. "I must go and get ready to play croquet with the Queen," and she hurried out of the room. The cook threw a frying-pan after her as she went, but it just missed her.

28

Alice caught the baby with some difficulty, as it was a queer-shaped little creature, and held out its arms and legs in all directions.

She carried it out into the open air. "If I don't take this child away with me," thought Alice, "they're sure to kill it in a day or two."

The baby grunted, and Alice looked very anxiously into its face to see what was the matter with it. There could be no doubt that it had a *very* turn-up nose, much more like a snout than a real nose: also its eyes were getting extremely small for a baby: altogether Alice did not like the look of the thing at all.

She was just beginning to think to herself, "Now, what am I to do with this creature, when I get it home?" when it grunted again, so violently, that she looked down into its face in some alarm. This time there could be *no* mistake about it: it was neither more nor less than a pig, and she felt that it would be quite absurd for her to carry it any further.

So she set the little creature down, and felt quite relieved to see it trot away quietly into the wood. "If it had grown up," she said to herself, "it would have made a dreadfully ugly child: but it makes rather a handsome pig, I think." And she began thinking over other children she knew, who might do very well as pigs, when she was a little startled by seeing the Cheshire-Cat sitting on a bough of a tree a few yards off.

The Cat only grinned when it saw Alice. It looked good-natured, she thought: still it had *very* long claws and a great many teeth, so she felt that it ought to be treated with respect.

"Cheshire-Puss," she began, rather timidly, "would you tell me, please, which way I ought to go from here?"

"That depends a good deal on where you want to get to," said the Cat.

"I don't much care where——" said Alice.

"Then it doesn't matter which way you go," said the Cat.

"——so long as I get *somewhere*," Alice added as an explanation.

"Oh, you're sure to do that," said the Cat, "if you only walk long enough."

Alice felt that this could not be denied, so she tried another question. "What sort of people live about here?"

"In *that* direction," the Cat said, waving its right paw round, "lives a Hatter: and in *that* direction," waving the other paw, "lives a March Hare. Visit either you like: they're both mad."

"But I don't want to go among mad people," Alice remarked.

"Oh, you can't help that," said the Cat: "we're all mad here. I'm mad. You're mad."

"How do you know I'm mad?" said Alice.

"You must be," said the Cat, "or you wouldn't have come here. Do you play croquet with the Queen to-day?"

"I should like it very much," said Alice, "but I haven't been invited yet."

"You'll see me there," said the Cat, and vanished.

Alice was not much surprised at this, she was getting so well used to queer things happening. While she was still looking at the place where it had been, it suddenly appeared again.

"By-the-bye, what became of the baby?" said the Cat. "I'd nearly forgotten to ask."

"It turned into a pig," Alice answered very quietly, just as if the Cat had come back in a natural way.

"I thought it would," said the Cat.

"I wish you wouldn't keep appearing and vanishing so suddenly," said Alice. "You make one quite giddy!"

"All right," said the Cat; and this time it vanished quite slowly, beginning with the end of the tail, and ending with the grin, which remained some time after the rest of it had gone.

"Well! I've often seen a cat without a grin," thought Alice; "but a grin without a cat! It's the most curious thing I ever saw in all my life!"

Alice walked on. She had not gone very far before she came in sight of the house of the March Hare: she thought it must be the right house, because the chimneys were shaped like ears and the roof was thatched with fur. It was so large a house, that she did not like to go nearer till she had nibbled some more of the left-hand bit of mushroom, and raised herself to about two feet high: even then she walked up towards it rather timidly, saying to herself, "Suppose it should be raving mad after all! I almost wish I'd gone to see the Hatter instead!"

7 A Mad Tea-Party

There was a table set out under a tree in front of the house, and the March Hare and the Hatter were having tea at it: a Dormouse was sitting between them, fast asleep, and the other two were using it as a cushion, resting their elbows on it, and talking over its head. "Very uncomfortable for the Dormouse," thought Alice; "only as it's asleep, I suppose it doesn't mind."

The table was a large one, but the three were all crowded together at one corner of it. "No room! No room!" they cried out when they saw Alice coming. "There's *plenty* of room!" said Alice indignantly, and she sat down in a large arm-chair at one end of the table.

"Have some wine," the March Hare said in an encouraging tone.

Alice looked all round the table, but there was nothing on it but tea. "I don't see any wine," she remarked.

"There isn't any," said the March Hare.

"Then it wasn't very civil of you to offer it," said Alice angrily.

"It wasn't very civil of you to sit down without being invited," said the March Hare.

"I didn't know it was *your* table," said Alice: "it's laid for a great many more than three."

"Your hair wants cutting," said the Hatter. He had been looking at Alice for some time with great curiosity, and this was his first speech.

"You should learn not to make personal remarks," Alice said with some severity: "It's very rude."

32

The Hatter opened his eyes very wide on hearing this; but all he *said* was, "Why is a raven like a writing-desk?"

"Come, we shall have some fun now!" thought Alice. "I'm glad they've begun asking riddles—I believe I can guess that," she added aloud.

"Do you mean that you think you can find out the answer to it?" said the March Hare.

"Exactly so," said Alice.

"Then you should say what you mean," the March Hare went on.

"I do," Alice hastily replied; "at least—at least I mean what I say—that's the same thing, you know."

"Not the same thing a bit!" said the Hatter. "Why, you might just as well say that 'I see what I eat' is the same thing as 'I eat what I see'!"

"You might just as well say," added the March Hare, "that 'I like what I get' is the same thing as 'I get what I like'!"

"You might just as well say," added the Dormouse, which seemed to be talking in its sleep, "that 'I breathe when I sleep' is the same thing as 'I sleep when I breathe'!"

"It *is* the same thing with you," said the Hatter, and here the conversation dropped, and the party sat silent for a minute, while Alice thought over all she could remember about ravens and writing-desks, which wasn't much.

"The Dormouse is asleep again," said the Hatter, and he poured a little hot tea upon its nose.

The Dormouse shook its head impatiently, and said, without opening its eyes, "Of course: just what I was going to remark myself."

"Have you guessed the riddle yet?" the Hatter said, turning to Alice again.

"No, I give it up," Alice replied. "What's the answer?"

"I haven't the slightest idea," said the Hatter.

"Nor I," said the March Hare.

Alice sighed wearily. "I think you might do something better with the time," she said, "than wasting it in asking riddles that have no answers."

"If you knew Time as well as I do," said the Hatter, "you wouldn't talk about wasting *it*. It's *him*."

"I don't know what you mean," said Alice.

"Of course you don't!" the Hatter said, tossing his head contemptuously. "I dare say you never even spoke to Time!"

"Perhaps not," Alice cautiously replied; "but I know I have to beat time when I learn music."

"Ah! That accounts for it," said the Hatter. "He won't stand beating. Now, if you only kept on good terms with him, he'd do almost anything you liked with the clock. For instance, suppose it were nine o'clock in the morning, just time to begin lessons: you'd only have to whisper a hint to Time, and round goes the clock in a twinkling! Half-past one, time for dinner!"

("I only wish it was," the March Hare said to itself in a whisper.)

"That would be grand, certainly," said Alice thoughtfully; "but then—I shouldn't be hungry for it, you know."

"Not at first, perhaps," said the Hatter: "but you could keep it to half-past one as long as you liked."

"Is that the way *you* manage?" Alice asked.

The Hatter shook his head mournfully. "Not I!" he replied. "We quarreled last March——just before *he* went mad, you know——" (pointing with his teaspoon at the March Hare,) "——it was at the great concert given by the Queen of Hearts, and I had to sing

'*Twinkle, twinkle, little bat!*
How I wonder what you're at!'

You know the song, perhaps?"

"I've heard something like it," said Alice.

"It goes on, you know," the Hatter continued, "in this way:

'*Up above the world you fly,*
Like a tea-tray in the sky.
Twinkle, twinkle——' "

Here the Dormouse shook itself, and began singing in its sleep *"Twinkle, twinkle, twinkle, twinkle*——" and went on so long that they had to pinch it to make it stop.

"Well, I'd hardly finished the first verse," said the Hatter, "when the Queen bawled out 'He's murdering the time! Off with his head!' "

"How dreadfully savage!" exclaimed Alice.

"And ever since that," the Hatter went on in a mournful tone, "he won't do a thing I ask! It's always six o'clock now."

A bright idea came into Alice's head. "Is that the reason so many tea-things are put out here?" she asked.

"Yes, that's it," said the Hatter with a sigh: "it's always tea-time, and we've no time to wash the things between whiles."

"Then you keep moving round, I suppose?" said Alice.

"Exactly so," said the Hatter: "as the things get used up."

"But what happens when you come to the beginning again?" Alice ventured to ask.

"Suppose we change the subject," the March Hare interrupted, yawning. "I'm getting tired of this. I vote the young lady tells us a story."

"I'm afraid I don't know one," said Alice, rather alarmed at the proposal.

"Then the Dormouse shall!" they both cried. "Wake up, Dormouse!" And they pinched it on both sides at once.

The Dormouse slowly opened its eyes. "I wasn't asleep," it said in a hoarse, feeble voice, "I heard every word you fellows were saying."

"Tell us a story!" said the March Hare.

"Yes, please do!" pleaded Alice.

"And be quick about it," added the Hatter, "or you'll be asleep again before it's done."

"Once upon a time there were three little sisters," the Dormouse began in a great hurry; "and their names were Elsie, Lacie, and Tillie; and they lived at the bottom of a well——"

"What did they live on?" said Alice, who always took a great interest in questions of eating and drinking.

"They lived on treacle," said the Dormouse, after thinking a minute or two.

"They couldn't have done that, you know," Alice gently remarked. "They'd have been ill."

"So they were," said the Dormouse; "*very* ill."

Alice tried a little to fancy to herself what such an extraordinary way of living would be like, but it puzzled her too much: so she went on: "But why did they live at the bottom of a well?"

"Take some more tea," the March Hare said to Alice, very earnestly.

"I've had nothing yet," Alice replied in an offended tone: "so I can't take more."

"You mean you can't take *less,*" said the Hatter: "it's very easy to take *more* than nothing."

"Nobody asked *your* opinion," said Alice.

"Who's making personal remarks now?" the Hatter asked triumphantly.

Alice did not quite know what to say to this: so she helped herself to some tea and bread-and-butter, and then turned to the Dormouse, and repeated her question. "Why did they live at the bottom of a well?"

The Dormouse again took a minute or two to think about it, and then said "It was a treacle-well."

"There's no such thing!" Alice was beginning very angrily, but the Hatter and the March Hare went "Sh! Sh!" and the Dormouse sulkily remarked "If you can't be civil, you'd better finish the story for yourself."

"No, please go on!" Alice said very humbly. "I won't interrupt you again. I dare say there may be *one*."

"One, indeed!" said the Dormouse indignantly. However, he consented to go on. "And so these three little sisters—they were learning to draw, you know——"

"What did they draw?" said Alice, quite forgetting her promise.

"Treacle," said the Dormouse, without considering at all, this time.

"I want a clean cup," interrupted the Hatter: "let's all move one place on."

He moved on as he spoke, and the Dormouse followed him: the March Hare moved into the Dormouse's place, and Alice rather unwillingly took the place of the March Hare. The Hatter was the only one who got any advantage from the change; and Alice was a good deal worse off than before, as the March Hare had just upset the milk-jug into his plate.

Alice did not wish to offend the Dormouse again, so she began very cautiously: "But I don't understand. Where did they draw the treacle from?"

"You can draw water out of a water-well," said the Hatter; "so I should think you could draw treacle out of a treacle-well—eh, stupid?"

"But they were *in* the well," Alice said to the Dormouse, not choosing to notice this last remark.

"Of course they were," said the Dormouse: "well in."

This answer so confused poor Alice, that she let the Dormouse go on for some time without interrupting it.

"They were learning to draw," the Dormouse went on, yawning and rubbing its eyes, for it was getting very sleepy; "and they drew all manner of things —everything that begins with an M——"

"Why with an M?" said Alice.

"Why not?" said the March Hare. Alice was silent.

The Dormouse had closed its eyes by this time, and was going off into a doze; but, on being pinched by the Hatter, it woke up again with a little shriek, and went on: "——that begins with an M, such as mouse-traps, and the moon, and memory, and muchness—you know you say things are 'much of a muchness'—did you ever see such a thing as a drawing of a muchness!"

"Really, now you ask me," said Alice, very much confused, "I don't think——"

"Then you shouldn't talk," said the Hatter.

This piece of rudeness was more than Alice could bear: she got up in great disgust, and walked off: the Dormouse fell asleep instantly, and neither of the others took the least notice of her going, though she looked back once or twice, half hoping that they would call after her: the last time she saw them, they were trying to put the Dormouse into the teapot.

"At any rate I'll never go *there* again!" said Alice, as she picked her way through the wood. "It's the stupidest tea-party I ever was at in all my life!"

Just as she said this, she noticed that one of the trees had a door leading right into it. "That's very curious!" she thought. "But everything's curious to-day. I think I may as well go in at once." And in she went.

Once more she found herself in the long hall, and close to the little glass table. "Now, I'll manage better this time," she said to herself, and began by taking the little golden key, and unlocking the door that led into the garden. Then she set to work nibbling at the mushroom (she had kept a piece of it in her pocket) till she was about a foot high: then she walked down the little passage: and *then*—she found herself at last in the beautiful garden, among the bright flower-beds and the cool fountains.

8   The Queen's Croquet Ground

A large rose-tree stood near the entrance of the garden: the roses growing on it were white, but there were three gardeners at it, busily painting them red. Alice thought this a very curious thing, and she went nearer to watch them, and, just as she came up to them, she heard one of them say "Look out now, Five! Don't go splashing paint over me like that!"

"I couldn't help it," said Five, in a sulky tone. "Seven jogged my elbow."

On which Seven looked up and said "That's right, Five! Always lay the blame on others!"

"*You'd* better not talk!" said Five. "I heard the Queen say only yesterday you deserved to be beheaded."

Seven flung down his brush, and had just begun "Well, of all the unjust things—" when his eye chanced to fall upon Alice, as she stood watching them, and he checked himself suddenly: the others looked round also, and all of them bowed low.

"Would you tell me, please," said Alice, a little timidly, "why you are painting those roses?"

Five and Seven said nothing, but looked at Two. Two began, in a low voice, "Why, the fact is, you see, Miss, this here ought to have been a *red* rose-tree, and we put a white one in by mistake; and, if the Queen was to find it out, we should all have our heads cut off, you know. So you see, Miss, we're doing our best, afore she comes, to—" At this moment, Five, who had been anxiously looking across the garden, called out "The Queen! The Queen!" and the three gardeners instantly threw themselves flat upon their faces. There was a sound of many footsteps, and Alice looked round, eager to see the Queen.

First came ten soldiers carrying clubs: these were all shaped like the three gardeners, oblong and flat, with their hands and feet at the corners: next the ten courtiers: these were ornamented all over with diamonds, and walked two and two, as the soldiers did. After these came the royal children: there were

ten of them, and the little dears came jumping merrily along, hand in hand, in couples: they were all ornamented with hearts. Next came the guests, mostly

40

Kings and Queens, and among them Alice recognized the White Rabbit: it was talking in a hurried nervous manner, smiling at everything that was said, and went by without noticing her. Then followed the Knave of Hearts, carrying the King's crown on a crimson velvet cushion; and, last of all this grand procession, came THE KING AND THE QUEEN OF HEARTS.

When the procession came opposite to Alice, they all stopped and looked at her, and the Queen said, severely, "Who is this?" She said it to the Knave of Hearts, who only bowed and smiled in reply.

"Idiot!" said the Queen, tossing her head impatiently; and, turning to Alice, she went on: "What's your name, child?"

"My name is Alice, so please your Majesty," said Alice very politely; but she added, to herself, "Why, they're only a pack of cards, after all. I needn't be afraid of them!"

"And who are *these*?" said the Queen, pointing to the three gardeners who were lying round the rose-tree; for, you see, as they were lying on their faces, and the pattern on their backs was the same as the rest of the pack, she could not tell whether they were gardeners, or soldiers, or courtiers, or three of her own children.

"How should *I* know?" said Alice, surprised at her own courage. "It's no business of *mine.*"

The Queen turned crimson with fury, and, after glaring at her for a moment like a wild beast, began screaming "Off with her head! Off with——"

"Nonsense!" said Alice, very loudly and decidedly, and the Queen was silent.

The King laid his hand upon her arm, and timidly said, "Consider, my dear: she is only a child!"

The Queen turned angrily away from him, and said to the Knave, "Turn them over!"

The Knave did so, very carefully, with one foot.

"Get up!" said the Queen in a shrill, loud voice, and the three gardeners instantly jumped up, and began bowing to the King, the Queen, the royal children, and everybody else.

"Leave off that!" screamed the Queen. "You make me giddy." And then, turning to the rose-tree, she went on "What *have* you been doing here?"

"May it please your Majesty," said Two, in a very humble tone, going down on one knee as he spoke, "we were trying——"

"*I* see!" said the Queen, who had meanwhile been examining the roses. "Off with their heads!" and the procession moved on, three of the soldiers remaining behind to execute the unfortunate gardeners, who ran to Alice for protection.

"You shan't be beheaded!" said Alice, and she put them into a large flower-pot that stood near. The three soldiers wandered about for a minute or two, looking for them, and then quietly marched off after the others.

"Are their heads off?" shouted the Queen.

"Their heads are gone, if it please your Majesty!" the soldiers shouted in reply.

"That's right!" shouted the Queen. "Can you play croquet?"

The soldiers were silent, and looked at Alice, as the question was evidently meant for her.

"Yes!" shouted Alice. "Come on, then!" roared the Queen, and Alice joined the procession, wondering very much what would happen next.

"It's—it's a very fine day!" said a timid voice at her side. She was walking by the White Rabbit, who was peeping anxiously into her face.

"Very," said Alice. "Where's the Duchess?"

"Hush! Hush!" said the Rabbit in a low hurried tone. He looked anxiously over his shoulder as he spoke, and then raised himself upon tiptoe, put his mouth close to her ear, and whispered, "She's under sentence of execution."

"What for?" said Alice.

"She boxed the Queen's ears—" the Rabbit began. Alice gave a little scream of laughter. "Oh, hush!" the Rabbit whispered in a frightened tone. "The Queen will hear you! You see she came rather late, and the Queen said—"

"Get to your places!" shouted the Queen in a voice of thunder, and people began running about in all directions, tumbling up against each other: however, they got settled down in a minute or two, and the game began.

Alice thought she had never seen such a curious croquet-ground in her life: it was all ridges and furrows: the croquet balls were live hedgehogs, and the mallets live flamingoes, and the soldiers had to double themselves up and stand on their hands and feet, to make the arches.

The players all played at once, without waiting for turns, quarreling all the while, and fighting for the hedgehogs; and in a very short time the Queen was in a furious passion, and went stamping about, and shouting "Off with his head!" or "Off with her head!" about once in a minute.

Alice began to feel very uneasy: to be sure, she had not as yet had any dispute with the Queen, but she knew that it might happen any minute, "and then," thought she, "what would become of me? They're dreadfully fond of beheading people here: the great wonder is, that there's any one left alive!"

She was looking about for some way of escape, and wondering whether she could get away without being seen, when she noticed a curious appearance in the air: it puzzled her very much at first, but after watching it a minute or two she made it out to be a grin, and she said to herself, "It's the Cheshire-Cat: now I shall have somebody to talk to."

"How are you getting on?" said the Cat, as soon as there was mouth enough for it to speak with.

"I don't think they play at all fairly," Alice began, in rather a complaining tone, "and they all quarrel so dreadfully one can't hear oneself speak—and they don't seem to have any rules in particular."

"How do you like the Queen?" said the Cat in a low voice.

"Not at all," said Alice: "she's so extremely—" Just then she noticed that the Queen was close behind her, listening: so she went on "—likely to win, that it's hardly worth while finishing the game."

The Queen smiled and passed on.

"Who *are* you talking to?" said the King, coming up to Alice, and looking at the Cat's head with great curiosity.

"It's a friend of mine—a Cheshire-Cat," said Alice: "allow me to introduce it."

"I don't like the look of it at all," said the King: "however, it may kiss my hand, if it likes."

"I'd rather not," the Cat remarked.

"Don't be impertinent," said the King, "and don't look at me like that!" He got behind Alice as he spoke.

"A cat may look at a king," said Alice. "I've read that in some book, but I don't remember where."

"Well, it must be removed," said the King very decidedly; and he called to the Queen, who was passing at the moment, "My dear! I wish you would have this cat removed!"

The Queen had only one way of settling all difficulties, great or small. "Off with his head!" she said without even looking around.

"I'll fetch the executioner myself," said the King eagerly, and he hurried off.

Alice thought she might as well go back and see how the game was going on, as she heard the Queen's voice in the distance, screaming with passion. She had already heard her sentence three of the players to be executed for having missed their turns, and she did not like the look of things at all, as the game was in such confusion that she never knew whether it was her turn or not. So she went back to have a little more conversation with her friend.

When she got back to the Cheshire-Cat, she was surprised to find quite a large crowd collected round it: there was a dispute going on between the executioner, the King, and the Queen, who were all talking at once, while all the rest were quite silent, and looked very uncomfortable.

The moment Alice appeared, she was appealed to by all three to settle the question, and they repeated their arguments to her, though, as they all spoke at once, she found it very hard to make out exactly what they said.

The executioner's argument was, that you couldn't cut off a head unless there was a body to cut it off from: that he had never had to do such a thing before, and he wasn't going to begin at *his* time of life.

The King's argument was that anything that had a head could be beheaded, and that you weren't to talk nonsense.

The Queen's argument was that, if something wasn't done about it in less than no time, she'd have everybody executed, all round. (It was this last remark that had made the whole party look so grave and anxious.)

Alice could think of nothing else to say but "It belongs to the Duchess: you'd better ask *her* about it."

"She's in prison," the Queen said to the executioner: "fetch her here." And the executioner went off like an arrow.

The Cat's head began fading away the moment he was gone, and, by the time he had come back with the Duchess, it had entirely disappeared: so the King and the executioner ran wildly up and down, looking for it, while the rest of the party went back to the game.

9   The Mock Turtle's Story

"You can't think how glad I am to see you again, you dear old thing!" said the Duchess, as she tucked her arm affectionately into Alice's, and they walked off together.

Alice did not much like her keeping so close to her: first because the Duchess was *very* ugly; and secondly, because she was exactly the right height to rest her chin on Alice's shoulder, and it was an uncomfortably sharp chin. However, she did not like to be rude: so she bore it as well as she could.

"The game's going on rather better now," she said, by way of keeping up the conversation a little.

" 'Tis so," said the Duchess: "and the moral of that is—'Oh, 'tis love, 'tis love, that makes the world go round!' "

"Somebody said," Alice whispered, "that it's done by everybody minding their own business!"

"Ah well! It means much the same thing," said the Duchess, digging her sharp little chin into Alice's shoulder as she added "and the moral of *that* is— 'Take care of the sense, and the sounds will take care of themselves.' "

"How fond she is of finding morals in things!" Alice thought to herself.

"Thinking?" the Duchess asked, with another dig of her sharp little chin.

"I've a right to think," said Alice sharply, for she was beginning to feel a little worried.

"Just about as much right," said the Duchess, "as pigs have to fly; and the m——"

But here, to Alice's great surprise, the Duchess's voice died away, even in the middle of her favorite word 'moral,' and the arm that was linked into hers began to tremble. Alice looked up, and there stood the Queen in front of them, with her arms folded, frowning like a thunderstorm.

"A fine day, your Majesty!" the Duchess began in a low, weak voice.

"Now, I give you fair warning," shouted the Queen, stamping on the ground as she spoke; "either you or your head must be off, and that in about half no time! Take your choice!"

The Duchess took her choice, and was gone in a moment.

"Let's go on with the game," the Queen said to Alice; and Alice was too much frightened to say a word, but slowly followed her back to the croquet-ground.

The other guests had taken advantage of the Queen's absence, and were resting in the shade: however, the moment they saw her, they hurried back to the game, the Queen merely remarking that a moment's delay would cost them their lives.

All the time they were playing the Queen never left off quarreling with the other players and shouting "Off with his head!" or "Off with her head!" Those whom she sentenced were taken into custody by the soldiers, who of course had to leave off being arches to do this, so that, by the end of half an hour or so, there were no arches left, and all the players, except the King, the Queen, and Alice, were in custody and under sentence of execution.

Then the Queen left off, quite out of breath, and said to Alice, "Have you seen the Mock Turtle yet?"

"No," said Alice. "I don't even know what a Mock Turtle is."

"It's the thing Mock Turtle Soup is made from," said the Queen.

"I never saw one, or heard of one," said Alice.

"Come on, then," said the Queen, "and he shall tell you his history."

As they walked off together, Alice heard the King say in a low voice, to the company, generally, "You are all pardoned." "Come, *that's* a good thing!" she said to herself, for she had felt quite unhappy at the number of executions the Queen had ordered.

They very soon came upon a Gryphon, lying fast asleep in the sun. "Up, lazy thing!" said the Queen, "and take this young lady to see the Mock Turtle, and to hear his history. I must go back and see after some executions I have ordered," and she walked off, leaving Alice alone with the Gryphon. Alice did not quite like the look of the creature, but on the whole she thought it would be quite as safe to stay with it as to go after that savage Queen: so she waited.

The Gryphon sat up and rubbed its eyes: then it watched the Queen till she was out of sight: then it chuckled. "What fun!" said the Gryphon, half to itself, half to Alice.

"What *is* the fun?" said Alice.

"Why, *she,*" said the Gryphon. "It's all her fancy, that: they never executes nobody, you know. Come on!"

"Everybody says 'come on!' here," thought Alice, as she went slowly after it: "I never was so ordered about before, in all my life, never!"

They had not gone far before they saw the Mock Turtle in the distance, sitting sad and lonely on a little ledge of rock, and, as they came nearer, Alice could hear him sighing as if his heart would break. She pitied him deeply. "What is his sorrow?" she asked the Gryphon. And the Gryphon answered, very nearly in the same words as before, "It's all his fancy, that: he hasn't got no sorrow, you know. Come on!"

So they went up to the Mock Turtle, who looked at them with large eyes full of tears, but said nothing.

"This here young lady," said the Gryphon, "she wants for to know your history, she do."

"I'll tell it her," said the Mock Turtle in a deep, hollow tone. "Sit down, both of you, and don't speak a word till I've finished."

So they sat down, and nobody spoke for some minutes. Alice thought to herself, "I don't see how he can *ever* finish, if he doesn't begin." But she waited patiently.

"Once," said the Mock Turtle at last, with a deep sigh, "I was a real Turtle. When we were little, we went to school in the sea. The master was an old Turtle —we used to call him Tortoise———"

"Why did you call him Tortoise, if he wasn't one?" Alice asked.

"We called him Tortoise because he taught us," said the Mock Turtle angrily. "Really you are very dull! Yes, we went to school in the sea, though you mayn't believe it. We had the best of educations—in fact, we went to school every day———"

"*I've* been to a day-school, too," said Alice. "You needn't be so proud as all that."

"With extras?" asked the Mock Turtle, a little anxiously.

"Yes," said Alice: "we learned French and music."

"And washing?" said the Mock Turtle.

"Certainly not!" said Alice indignantly.

"Ah! Then yours wasn't a really good school," said the Mock Turtle in a tone of great relief. "Now, at *ours,* they had, at the end of the bill, 'French, music, *and washing*—extra.'"

"You couldn't have wanted it much," said Alice; "living at the bottom of the sea."

"I couldn't afford to learn it," said the Mock Turtle with a sigh. "I only took the regular course."

"What was that?" inquired Alice.

"Reeling and Writhing, of course, to begin with," the Mock Turtle replied; "and then the different branches of Arithmetic—Ambition, Distraction, Uglification, and Derision."

"And how many hours a day did you do lessons?" said Alice.

"Ten hours the first day," said the Mock Turtle: "nine the next, and so on."

"What a curious plan!" exclaimed Alice.

"That's the reason they're called lessons," the Gryphon remarked: "because they lessen from day to day."

This was quite a new idea to Alice, and she thought it over a little before she made her next remark. "Then the eleventh day must have been a holiday?"

"Of course it was," said the Mock Turtle.

"And how did you manage on the twelfth?" Alice went on eagerly.

"That's enough about lessons," the Gryphon interrupted in a very decided tone. "Would you like the Mock Turtle to sing you a song?"

"Oh, a song, please, if the Mock Turtle would be so kind," Alice replied, so eagerly that the Gryphon said, "Sing her '*Turtle Soup*,' will you, old fellow?"

The Mock Turtle sighed deeply, and began in a voice choked with sobs, to sing this:

> *"Beautiful Soup, so rich and green,*
> *Waiting in a hot tureen!*
> *Who for such dainties would not stoop?*
> *Soup of the evening, beautiful Soup!*
> *Soup of the evening, beautiful Soup!*
> *Beau—ootiful Soo—oop!*
> *Beau—ootiful Soo—oop!*
> *Soo—oop of the e—e—evening,*
> *Beautiful, beautiful Soup!"*

"Chorus again!" cried the Gryphon, and the Mock Turtle had just begun to repeat it, when a cry of "The trial's beginning!" was heard in the distance.

"Come on!" cried the Gryphon, and, taking Alice by the hand, it hurried off, without waiting for the end of the song.

"What trial is it?" Alice panted as she ran: but the Gryphon only answered "Come on!" and ran the faster, while more and more faintly came, carried on the breeze that followed them, the melancholy words:

> *"Soo—oop of the e—e—evening,*
> *Beautiful, beautiful Soup!"*

10 Who Stole the Tarts?

The King and Queen of Hearts were seated on their throne when they arrived, with a great crowd assembled about them—all sorts of little birds and beasts, as well as the whole pack of cards: the Knave was standing before them, in chains, with a soldier on each side to guard him; and near the King was the White Rabbit, with a trumpet in one hand, and a scroll of parchment in the other. In the very middle of the court was a table, with a large dish of tarts upon it: they looked so good, that it made Alice quite hungry to look at them— "I wish they'd get the trial done," she thought, "and hand round the refreshments!" But there seemed to be no chance of this; so she began looking at everything about her to pass away the time.

Alice had never been in a court of justice before, but she had read about them in books, and she was quite pleased to find that she knew the name of nearly everything there. "That's the judge," she said to herself, "because of his great wig."

The judge, by the way, was the King; and, as he wore his crown over the wig, he did not look at all comfortable, and it was certainly not becoming.

"And that's the jury-box," thought Alice; "and those twelve creatures," (she was obliged to say "creatures," you see, because some of them were animals, and some were birds,) "I suppose they are the jurors."

The twelve jurors were all writing very busily on slates. "What are they doing?" Alice whispered to the Gryphon. "They can't have anything to put down yet, before the trial's begun."

"They're putting down their names," the Gryphon whispered in reply, "for fear they should forget them before the end of the trial."

"Stupid things!" Alice began in a loud indignant voice; but she stopped herself hastily, for the White Rabbit cried out "Silence in the court!" and the King put on his spectacles and looked anxiously round, to make out who was talking.

"Herald, read the accusation!" said the King.

On this the White Rabbit blew three blasts on the trumpet, and then unrolled the parchment-scroll, and read as follows:

"The Queen of Hearts, she made some tarts,
        All on a summer day:
    The Knave of Hearts, he stole those tarts
        And took them quite away!"

"Consider your verdict," the King said to the jury.

"Not yet, not yet!" the Rabbit hastily interrupted. "There's a great deal to come before that!"

"Call the first witness," said the King; and the White Rabbit blew three blasts on the trumpet, and called out, "First witness!"

The first witness was the Hatter. He came in with a teacup in one hand and a piece of bread-and-butter in the other. "I beg pardon, your Majesty," he began, "for bringing these in; but I hadn't quite finished my tea when I was sent for."

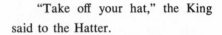

"Take off your hat," the King said to the Hatter.

"It isn't mine," said the Hatter.

"Stolen!" the King exclaimed, turning to the jury, who instantly made a memorandum of the fact.

"I keep them to sell," the Hatter added as an explanation. "I've none of my own. I'm a hatter."

"Give your evidence," said the King; "and don't be nervous, or I'll have you executed on the spot."

This did not seem to encourage the witness at all: he kept shifting from one foot to the other, and in his confusion he bit a large piece out of his teacup instead of the bread-and-butter.

Just at this moment Alice felt a very curious sensation, which puzzled her a good deal until she made out what it was: she was beginning to grow larger again, and she thought at first she would get up and leave the court; but on second thought she decided to remain where she was as long as there was room for her.

"I wish you wouldn't squeeze so," said the Dormouse, who was sitting next to her. "I can hardly breathe."

"I can't help it," said Alice very meekly: "I'm growing."

"You've no right to grow *here,*" said the Dormouse.

"Don't talk nonsense," said Alice more boldly: "you know you're growing too."

"Yes, but *I* grow at a reasonable pace," said the Dormouse: "not in that ridiculous fashion." And he got up very sulkily and crossed over to the other side of the court.

"I'm a poor man, your Majesty," the Hatter began, in a trembling voice, "and I hadn't but just begun my tea—not above a week or so—and what with the bread-and-butter getting so thin—I'm a poor man, your Majesty," he said again.

"You're a *very* poor *speaker,*" said the King. "You may stand down."

"I can't go no lower," said the Hatter: "I'm on the floor, as it is."

"Then you may *sit* down," the King replied. "Call the next witness!"

Alice watched the White Rabbit as he fumbled over the list, feeling very curious to see what the next witness would be like, "—for they haven't got much evidence *yet,*" she said to herself. Imagine her surprise, when the White Rabbit read out, at the top of his shrill little voice, the name "Alice!"

11 Alice's Evidence

"Here!" cried Alice, quite forgetting in the flurry of the moment how large she had grown in the last few minutes, and she jumped up in such a hurry that she tipped over the jury-box with the edge of her skirt, upsetting all the jury-men on to the heads of the crowd below, and there they lay sprawling about.

"Oh, I *beg* your pardon!" she exclaimed in a tone of great dismay, and began picking them up again as quickly as she could.

"The trial cannot proceed," said the King, in a very grave voice, "until all the jurymen are back in their proper places—*all,*" he repeated with great emphasis, looking hard at Alice as he said so.

Alice looked at the jury-box, and saw that, in her haste, she had put the Lizard in head downwards, and the poor little thing was waving its tail about in a melancholy way, being quite unable to move. She soon got it out again, and put it right.

"What do you know about this business?" the King said to Alice.

"Nothing," said Alice.

"Nothing *whatever?*" persisted the King.

"Nothing whatever," said Alice.

At this moment the King called out "Silence!" and read out from his book, "Rule Forty-two. *All persons more than a mile high to leave the court.*"

Everybody looked at Alice.

"*I'm* not a mile high," said Alice.

"You are," said the King.

"Nearly two miles high," added the Queen.

"Well, I shan't go, at any rate," said Alice.

The King turned pale, and shut his note-book hastily. "Consider your verdict," he said to the jury, in a low trembling voice.

"There's more evidence to come yet, please your Majesty," said the White Rabbit, jumping up in a great hurry: "this paper has just been picked up."

"What's in it?" said the Queen.

"I haven't opened it yet," said the White Rabbit; "but it seems to be a letter, written by the prisoner to—to somebody."

"It must have been that," said the King, "unless it was written to nobody, which isn't usual, you know."

"Who is it directed to?" said one of the jurymen.

"It isn't directed at all," said the White Rabbit: "in fact, there's nothing written on the *outside*." He unfolded the paper as he spoke, and added, "It isn't a letter, after all: it's a set of verses."

"Are they in the prisoner's handwriting?" asked another of the jurymen.

"No, they're not," said the White Rabbit, "and that's the queerest thing about it." (The jury all looked puzzled.)

"He must have imitated somebody else's hand," said the King. (The jury all brightened up again.)

"Please, your Majesty," said the Knave, "I didn't write it, and they can't prove that I did: there's no name signed at the end."

"If you didn't sign it," said the King, "that only makes the matter worse. You *must* have meant some mischief, or else you'd have signed your name like an honest man."

There was a general clapping of hands at this: it was the first really clever thing the King had said that day.

"That *proves* his guilt, of course," said the Queen: "so, off with——"

"It doesn't prove anything of the sort!" said Alice. "Why, you don't even know what they're about!"

"Read them," said the King.

The White Rabbit put on his spectacles. "Where shall I begin, please your Majesty?" he asked.

"Begin at the beginning," the King said, very gravely, "and go on till you come to the end: then stop."

There was dead silence in the court, whilst the White Rabbit read out these verses:

"They told me you had been to her,
　　And mentioned me to him:
She gave me a good character,
　　But said I could not swim.

"I gave her one, they gave him two,
　　You gave us three or more;
They all returned from him to you,
　　Though they were mine before.

"My notion was that you had been
   (Before she had this fit)
An obstacle that came between
   Him, and ourselves, and it.

"He sent them word I had not gone
   (We know it to be true):
If she should push the matter on,
   What would become of you?

"If I or she should chance to be
   Involved in this affair,
He trusts to you to set them free,
   Exactly as we were.

"Don't let him know she liked them best,
   For this must ever be
A secret, kept from all the rest,
   Between yourself and me."

"That's the most important piece of evidence we've heard yet," said the King, rubbing his hands; "so now let the jury——"

"If any one of them can explain it," said Alice, (she had grown so large in the last few minutes that she wasn't a bit afraid of interrupting him,) "I'll give him sixpence. *I* don't believe there's an atom of meaning in it."

The jury all wrote down, on their slates, *"She* doesn't believe there's an atom of meaning in it," but none of them attempted to explain the paper.

"If there's no meaning in it," said the King, "that saves a world of trouble, you know, as we needn't try to find any. And yet I don't know," he went on, spreading out the verses on his knee, and looking at them with one eye; "I

seem to see some meaning in them, after all. '—*said I could not swim*—' you can't swim, can you?" he added, turning to the Knave.

The Knave shook his head sadly. "Do I look like it?" he said. (Which he certainly did *not,* being made entirely of cardboard.)

"All right, so far," said the King; and he went on muttering over the verses to himself: " '*We know it to be true*'—that's the jury, of course—'*If she should push the matter on*'—that must be the Queen—'*What would become of you?*'— What, indeed!—'*I gave her one, they gave him two*'—why, that must be what he did with the tarts, you know——"

"But it goes on '*They all returned from him to you,*'" said Alice.

"Why, there they are!" said the King triumphantly, pointing to the tarts on the table. "Nothing can be clearer than *that.* Then again—'*before she had this fit*'—you never had *fits,* my dear, I think?" he said to the Queen.

"Never!" said the Queen, furiously, throwing an inkstand at the Lizard as she spoke.

"Then the words don't *fit* you," said the King, looking round the court with a smile. There was a dead silence.

"It's a pun!" the King added in an angry tone, and everybody laughed. "Let the jury consider their verdict," the King said, for about the twentieth time that day.

"No, no!" said the Queen. "Sentence first—verdict afterwards."

"Stuff and nonsense!" said Alice. "The idea of having the sentence first!"

"Hold your tongue!" said the Queen, turning purple.

"I won't!" said Alice.

"Off with her head!" the Queen shouted at the top of her voice. Nobody moved.

"Who cares for *you?*" said Alice (she had grown to her full size by this time). "You're nothing but a pack of cards!"

At this the whole pack rose up into the air, and came flying down upon her; she gave a little scream, half of fright and half of anger, and tried to beat them off,

This Book Belongs To
Tony and Nicole

Peter Pan

Edited by Josette Frank from PETER PAN and WENDY* by J. M. BARRIE

Illustrated by MARJORIE TORREY

RANDOM HOUSE · NEW YORK

Did you know that this book is part of the J. M. Barrie "Peter Pan Bequest"? This means that Sir J. M. Barrie's royalty on this book goes to The Hospital for Sick Children, Great Ormond Street, London, W. C. 1. to help the Hospital in its work for sick children.

1. Peter Breaks Through

The Darling family lived at number 14. There were Mr. and Mrs. Darling and their three children. Wendy was the oldest, then came John, then little Michael. There was nothing out of the ordinary about the Darling family; they were just like any of the other families that lived on their street, except for one thing. They employed a big Newfoundland dog as a nursemaid for their children. She was called Nana. The Darlings had found her in Kensington Gardens.

Mrs. Darling always said that Nana was a "treasure"; but Mr. Darling was a little afraid the neighbors might think it odd to have a dog for a nurse. Nana loved the children dearly, and took the best care of them, giving them their baths and making sure they took their medicine. Of course, her kennel was in the nursery, and she was up at any moment of the night if one of her charges made the slightest cry.

There was never a simpler, happier family, until the coming of Peter Pan. That was the night on which the extraordinary adventures of these children began.

It happened to be Nana's evening off, and Mrs. Darling had bathed the children and tucked them snugly into their beds. One by one they had slid into the land of sleep. Then Mrs. Darling had sat down by the fire to sew. But the fire was warm and the lights were dim, and soon her head was nodding and she, too, was asleep.

She was asleep and having a troubled dream about her children when the window of the nursery blew open and a boy dropped quietly to the floor. At the same time a strange light, no bigger than a child's fist, darted about the room like a living thing. It must have

been this light that awakened Mrs. Darling. She started up with a cry and saw the boy. He was a lovely boy, clad in skeleton leaves and the juices that ooze out of trees. When he saw that Mrs. Darling was a grownup he gnashed his teeth at her.

Mrs. Darling screamed, and, as if in answer to a bell, the door opened and Nana entered, returning from her night out. She growled and sprang at the boy, who leaped lightly through the window. Again Mrs. Darling screamed, this time in distress for him. She thought he must have been killed, for the nursery was on the third floor. She ran down into the street to look for him, but he was not there. She looked up, and in the black night she could see nothing but what she thought was a shooting star.

She returned to the nursery, and found Nana with something in her mouth which proved to be the boy's shadow. For, as he had jumped, Nana had closed the window quickly. She had been too late to catch him; but his shadow had not had time to get out. Slam went the window and the shadow was left behind.

Nana had no doubt of what was the best thing to do with this shadow. She hung it out of the window, meaning "He is sure to come back for it; let us put it where he can get it easily without disturbing the children."

But unfortunately Mrs. Darling could not leave it hanging out of the window; it looked so like the washing. She decided to roll it up and put it away carefully in a drawer until a fitting opportunity came for telling her husband about it. Ah me! The opportunity came a week later, on that never-to-be-forgotten Friday.

That Friday evening had begun uneventfully, exactly like a hundred other evenings. It happened that Mr. and Mrs. Darling were going out to dinner. Nana had bathed the children and got them ready for bed, and they were playing happily in the nursery. Mrs. Darling had come in, wearing her white evening gown. She had dressed early because Wendy loved to see her in her evening gown.

4

Suddenly Mr. Darling came rushing into the nursery with a crumpled tie in his hand.

"Why, what is the matter, Father dear?" Wendy asked.

"Matter!" he yelled; he really yelled. "This tie, it will not tie. Not around my neck! Around the bed post, yes; twenty times! But around my neck, no!"

"Let me try, dear," said Mrs. Darling, and with her nice cool hands she tied his tie for him. Mr. Darling thanked her, at once forgot his rage, and in another moment was dancing around the room with Michael on his back.

When the romp was over, Mrs. Darling felt this was an opportunity for telling her husband about the boy. At first he pooh-poohed the story, but he became thoughtful when she showed him the shadow.

"It is nobody I know," he said, examining it carefully, "but he does look a scoundrel."

They were still discussing it when Nana came in. Most unluckily she rubbed against Mr. Darling, covering his trousers with hair. He was very angry. Of course Mrs. Darling brushed him, but he began to talk again about its being a mistake to have a dog for a nurse. "I refuse to allow that dog in my nursery for an hour longer."

The children wept, and Nana ran to him beseechingly. But he waved her back. "The proper place for you is in the yard, and there you go to be tied up this instant."

"George, George," Mrs. Darling warned him. "Remember what I told you about that boy."

Alas, he would not listen. He was determined to show who was master in that house; he seized Nana roughly, and dragged her from the nursery.

In the meantime Mrs. Darling had put the children to bed in unusual silence, and lit their night-lights. They could hear Nana barking, and John whimpered, "It is because he is chaining her up in the yard." But Wendy was wiser.

"That is not Nana's unhappy bark," she said, little guessing what was about to happen. "That is her bark when she smells danger."

Danger!

Mrs. Darling quivered and went to the window. It was securely fastened. A nameless fear clutched at her heart and made her cry, "Oh, how I wish that I weren't going to a party tonight!"

Even Michael, already half asleep, knew that she was troubled, and he asked, "Can anything harm us, Mother, after the night-lights are lit?"

"Nothing, precious," she said. "They are the eyes a mother leaves behind her to guard her children."

She went from bed to bed, and little Michael threw his arms around her. "Mother," he cried, "I'm glad of you." They were the last words she was to hear from him for a long time.

2. Come Away, Come Away!

For a moment after Mr. and Mrs. Darling left the house the night-lights by the beds of the three children continued to burn clearly. Suddenly the lights blinked, and then went out.

There was another light in the room now, a thousand times brighter than the night-lights. In no time it had been in all the drawers in the nursery, looking for Peter's shadow, and had rummaged the wardrobe and turned every pocket inside out. It was not really a light. It made this light by flashing so quickly, but when it came to rest you saw that it was a girl fairy, no larger than your hand. She was called Tinker Bell.

A moment after the fairy's entrance, the window was blown open by the breathing of the little stars, and Peter dropped in.

"Tinker Bell," he called softly, after making sure that the children were asleep. "Tink, where are you?" She was in a jug for the moment, and liking it extremely; she had never been in a jug before.

"Oh, do come out of that jug, and tell me, do you know where they put my shadow?"

The loveliest tinkle as of golden bells answered him. It is the fairy language. Tink said the shadow was in the big chest, and Peter jumped at the drawers, scattering their contents on the floor with both hands. In a moment he had found his shadow, and in his delight he forgot that he had shut Tinker Bell up in a drawer.

No doubt he thought that he and his shadow, when brought near each other, would join like drops of water; and when this didn't happen he was terribly upset. He tried to stick the shadow on with soap from the bathroom, but that also failed. Peter sat on the floor and cried.

His sobs woke Wendy, and she sat up in bed. She was not alarmed to see a stranger crying on the nursery floor.

"Boy," she said courteously, "why are you crying?"

Peter could be very polite also; he rose and bowed to her beautifully. Wendy was much pleased, and bowed beautifully to him from the bed.

"What's your name?" he asked.

"Wendy Moira Angela Darling," she replied. "What is your name?"

"Peter Pan."

"Is that all?"

"Yes," he said rather sharply.

She asked where he lived.

"Second to the right," said Peter, "and then straight on till morning."

"What a funny address!" Wendy said nicely. "Is that what they put on the letters?"

"Don't get any letters," he said contemptuously.

"But your mother gets letters?"

"Don't have a mother," he said.

"Oh Peter, no wonder you were crying," she said, and got out of bed and ran to him.

"I wasn't crying about mothers," he said, rather indignantly. "I was crying because I can't get my shadow to stick on. Besides, I wasn't crying."

"It has come off?"

"Yes."

"How awful," Wendy said. But she could not help smiling when she saw that he had been trying to stick it on with soap. How exactly like a boy!

Fortunately she knew exactly what to do. "I shall sew it on for you." And she got out her sewing box and started to sew the shadow to Peter's foot.

10

"I daresay it will hurt a little," she warned him.

"Oh, I sha'n't cry," said Peter. And he clenched his teeth and did not cry, and soon his shadow was behaving properly, though it was still a little creased.

Now Peter jumped about in the wildest glee. He had already forgotten that he owed his joy to Wendy. He thought he had attached the shadow himself. "How clever I am," he crowed. "Oh, the cleverness of me!"

"Well," said Wendy indignantly, "if I am no use I can at least withdraw." And she sprang into bed and covered her face with the blankets.

"Wendy," said Peter, "don't withdraw." Then, when she showed no sign of coming out, he said, "Wendy, I think one girl is of more use than twenty boys."

"I think it's perfectly sweet of you," Wendy declared, "and I'll get up again." She sat on the side of the bed and said she would give him a kiss if he liked. Peter did not know what she meant, and he held out his hand.

"Surely you know what a kiss is?" she asked, aghast.

"I shall know when you give it to me," he replied stiffly; and not to hurt his feelings, Wendy took the thimble from her finger and gave it to him.

"Now," said he, "shall I give you a kiss?"

"If you please," she replied primly, and held her face toward him. But he merely dropped an acorn button into her hand. So she said nicely that she would wear his kiss on the chain around her neck. It was lucky that she did put it on that chain, for it was afterward to save her life.

Now Wendy asked Peter many questions, and his answers filled her with surprise. How strange that he didn't know how old he was! "I ran away the day I was born," he explained. "It was because I heard Father and Mother talking about what I was to be when I

12

became a man." Then, with great passion: "I don't want ever to be a man! I want always to be a little boy and to have fun. So I ran away to Kensington Gardens and lived a long time among the fairies."

Oh, did he really know fairies? Wendy poured out questions about them. Peter told her about the beginning of fairies.

"You see, Wendy, when the first baby laughed for the first time, its laugh broke into a thousand pieces, and they all went skipping about, and that was the beginning of fairies. And so there ought to be one fairy for every boy and girl; but there isn't. Because every time a child says 'I don't believe in fairies,' there is a fairy somewhere that falls down dead."

Now suddenly it struck him that Tinker Bell was keeping very quiet. "I can't think where she's gone to," he said.

"Peter," cried Wendy, "you don't mean to tell me there is a fairy in this room!"

There was a faint sound, like the tinkle of bells. The sound came from the chest of drawers.

"I do believe I shut her up in the drawer!" Peter whispered. He let poor Tink out of the drawer, and she flew about the nursery screaming with fury. "You shouldn't say such things," said Peter. "Of course I'm very sorry, but how could I know you were in the drawer?"

There were some angry bell tinkles.

"What is she saying now, Peter?" Wendy asked.

"She is not very polite. She says you are a great ugly girl, and that she is my fairy." He tried to argue with Tink, but she disappeared into the bathroom.

Now Wendy plied Peter with more questions. "If you don't live in Kensington Gardens now, where do you live mostly?"

"With the lost boys."

"Who are they?"

"They are the children who fall out of their carriages when the nursemaid is looking the other way. If they aren't claimed in seven days they are sent far away to the Neverland. I'm captain."

"What fun it must be!" said Wendy.

"Yes," said Peter, "but we are rather lonely, for there are no girls. Girls, you know, are far too clever to fall out of their carriages."

This flattered Wendy immensely. "I think," she said, "it is perfectly lovely, the way you talk about girls; so you may give me a kiss." For the moment she had forgotten his ignorance about kisses.

"I thought you'd be wanting it back," Peter said, and offered to return the thimble.

"Oh dear," said Wendy, "I don't mean a kiss, I mean a thimble."

"What's that?"

"It's like this." She kissed him.

"Funny," said Peter gravely. "Now shall I give you a thimble?"

"If you wish to," said Wendy.

Peter thimbled her, and almost immediately she screeched.

"What is it, Wendy?"

"It was exactly as if someone were pulling my hair."

"That must have been Tink." And indeed Tink was darting about again, using offensive language.

"She says she will do that to you, Wendy, every time I give you a thimble."

14

Peter could not understand why, but Wendy understood. And she was slightly disappointed when Peter admitted that he had come to the nursery window not to see her but to listen to stories.

"None of the lost boys know any stories," he said. "And oh, Wendy, your mother was telling such a lovely story about the prince who couldn't find the lady who wore the glass slipper."

"That was *Cinderella*," said Wendy excitedly, "and, Peter, he found her and they lived happily ever after."

Peter rose quickly from the floor and hurried to the window.

"Where are you going?" Wendy cried.

"To tell the other boys."

"Don't go, Peter," she begged. "I know lots of stories."

Now Peter came back, and there was a greedy look in his eyes. He gripped her and began to draw her toward the window. "Wendy, do come with me and tell the other boys."

"Oh dear, I can't. Think of Mummy! Besides, I can't fly."

"I'll teach you," Peter promised.

"Oh, how lovely to fly!"

"I'll teach you to jump on the wind's back, and then away we go."

"Oo!" Wendy exclaimed rapturously.

"Wendy, you could tuck us in at night. None of us has ever been tucked in at night. And you could darn our clothes and make pockets for us. None of us has any pockets."

How could she resist? "It's awfully fascinating!" she cried. "Would you teach John and Michael to fly too?"

"If you like," Peter said; and Wendy ran to John and Michael and shook them. "Wake up!" she cried. "Peter Pan has come and he's going to teach us to fly."

John rubbed his eyes and sat up. "I say, Peter, can you really fly?" Instead of answering him Peter flew around the room, stepping onto

the mantelpiece on the way.

It looked delightfully easy and the children tried it, first from the floor and then from the beds, but they always went down instead of up.

"I say, how do you do it?" asked John, rubbing his knee.

"You just think lovely thoughts and they lift you up in the air," Peter told them. And he showed them again. But not one of them could fly an inch.

Of course, Peter had been fooling them, for no one can fly unless the fairy dust has been blown on him. Fortunately, Peter had some on one of his hands, and he blew some on each of them. "Now just wriggle your shoulders this way," he said, "and let go."

They were all on their beds, and Michael let go first. Immediately he was borne across the room. "I flewed!" he screamed. Then John let go and met Wendy near the bathroom. "Look at me!" "Look at me!" Up and down they went and around and around.

"I say," cried John, "why shouldn't we all go out?" Of course it was to this that Peter had been luring them. Michael was ready. But Wendy hesitated.

"There are mermaids!" said Peter.

"Oo!" cried Wendy. "To see a mermaid!"

"And pirates," added Peter.

"Pirates!" cried John, seizing his Sunday hat. "Let us go at once."

It was just at this moment that Mr. and Mrs. Darling, coming home from the party, opened the street door. They would have reached the nursery in time had it not been that the little stars were watching them. Once again the stars blew the window open and the smallest star of all called out: "Cave, Peter!"

Then Peter knew that there was not a moment to lose.

"Come," he cried, and soared out at once into the night, followed by John and Michael and Wendy.

Mr. and Mrs. Darling and Nana rushed into the nursery, but they were too late. The birds had flown.

18

3. The Flight

"Second to the right, and straight on till morning."

That, Peter had told Wendy, was the way to the Neverland. But even birds could not have sighted it with these instructions. Peter, you see, just said anything that came into his head.

The children flew for a long time—they did not know how long. Sometimes it was dark and sometimes light. Sometimes they were very cold and again too warm. Sometimes they knew they were flying over the sea. When they grew tired or sleepy Peter showed them how to lie flat on a strong wind, and that was such a pleasant change that they tried it several times. Indeed they would have slept longer, but Peter tired quickly of sleeping, and soon he would cry in his captain voice, "We get off here." With so little sleep, they were weary as they drew near the Neverland.

"There it is," said Peter calmly.

"Where, where?" the children wanted to know.

"Where all the arrows are pointing."

And indeed a million golden arrows were pointing out the island to the children, all directed by their friend the Sun, who wanted them to be sure of their way before leaving them for the night.

But now fear fell upon the children, for the arrows faded, leaving the island in gloom. They had been flying apart, but they huddled close to Peter now. His careless manner was gone too. They were now flying so low that sometimes a tree grazed their feet. Nothing horrid was visible in the air, yet their progress had become slow and labored, exactly as if they were pushing their way through hostile forces. Sometimes Peter had to beat on the air with his fists.

"They don't want us to land," he explained. He did not explain who "they" were. Tinker Bell had been asleep on his shoulder, but now he wakened her and sent her on in front.

Sometimes Peter poised himself in the air, listening with his hand to his ear, and again he would stare down with eyes so bright they seemed to bore two holes to earth. His courage was almost appalling.

"Do you want an adventure?" he said casually to John. "There's a pirate asleep in the pampas just beneath us. If you like we'll go down and kill him."

"Suppose," John said, after a little pause, "he were to wake up."

Peter spoke indignantly. "You don't suppose I would kill him while he was sleeping! I would wake him first, and then kill him. That's the way I always do."

"I say! Do you kill many?"

"I kill tons of them," Peter boasted.

John asked if there were many pirates on the island just now, and Peter said he had never known so many.

"Who is captain now?"

"Hook," answered Peter; and his face became very stern as he said that hated name.

"James Hook?"

"Ay," answered Peter, looking grimmer than ever.

Then Michael began to cry, and even John could speak in gulps only, for they knew Hook's reputation. "He is the worst of them all," John whispered huskily. "What is he like? Is he big?"

"He is not so big as he was," Peter said.

"How do you mean?"

"I cut off a bit of him."

"You!"

"Yes, me," said Peter sharply.

"But, what bit?"

"His right hand."

"Then he can't fight now?" said John.

"Oh, can't he just!" Peter answered. "He has an iron hook instead of a right hand, and he claws with it."

"Claws!"

"I say, John," said Peter, "there is one thing that every boy who serves under me has to promise, and so must you."

John paled.

"It is this," Peter went on. "If we meet Hook in open fight you must leave him to me."

"I promise," John said loyally.

For the moment they were feeling less scary, because Tink was flying with them, and in her light they could see one another. Unfortunately she could not fly so slowly as they, and so she had to go around and around in a circle. Wendy liked this, but Peter pointed out that the pirates below, seeing her light, would guess they were near the island. The pirates had got out their big gun, Long Tom.

"If only one of us had a pocket," Peter said, "we could carry her in it."

However they had set out in such a hurry that there was not a pocket among the four of them.

Then Peter had a happy idea. John's hat! Tink agreed to travel by hat, if it was carried in the hand. She had hoped to be carried by Peter. But first John carried the hat, and then Wendy took it, and this led to mischief.

For a while they flew on in silence.

Suddenly the air was rent by a tremendous crash. The pirates had fired Long Tom at them. No one was hit, but Peter was carried by the force of the shot far out to sea, while Wendy was blown upward with no companion but Tinker Bell.

It would have been well for Wendy if at that moment she had dropped the hat, for Tink suddenly popped out of it and began to lure Wendy to her destruction. Tink was not all bad; but at that moment she was full of jealousy of Wendy. What she said in her lovely tinkle Wendy could not of course understand. Some of it was bad, but it sounded kind, and she flew backward and forward, plainly meaning "Follow me, and all will be well."

What else could poor Wendy do? She called to Peter and John and Michael and got only mocking echoes in reply. And so, bewildered, and now staggering in her flight, she followed Tink to her doom.

4. The Island Come True

Feeling that Peter was on his way back, the island had awakened into life. In his absence things usually were quiet on the island, but now one had only to put one's ear to the ground to hear the whole island seething with life.

On this evening the chief forces of the island were disposed as follows. The lost boys were out looking for Peter, the pirates were out looking for the lost boys, the Indians were out looking for the pirates, and the beasts were out looking for the Indians. They were going around and around the island, but they did not meet because all were going at the same rate.

All wanted blood except the boys, who tonight were out to greet their captain. There were six of them, counting the twins as two. They were forbidden by Peter to look in the least like him, and they wore the skins of animals slain by themselves. First there was Tootles, who had a kind sweet nature, and had been in fewer adventures than the others. Then there was Nibs, who was gay and light-hearted, and Slightly, who was the most conceited of the boys. The fourth was Curly, who was

always in some trouble or other, and last were the twins, who always kept close together.

The first to fall out of the circle moving around the island were the boys. They flung themselves down on the grass, close to their underground home.

"I do wish Peter would come back," every one of them said nervously.

"I am the only one who is not afraid of the pirates," Slightly said. "But I wish Peter would come back and tell us whether he has heard anything more about Cinderella."

While they talked they heard a distant sound. It was a grim song:

> Yo ho, yo ho, the pirate life,
> The flag o' skull and bones,
> A merry hour, a hempen rope,
> And hey for Davy Jones.

At once the lost boys were no longer there. Rabbits could not have disappeared more quickly. With the exception of Nibs, who had darted away to keep watch, they were already in their home under the ground. How had they reached it? On the ground above were seven large trees each having in its trunk a hole as large as a boy. These were the seven entrances to the home under the ground for which Hook had been searching in vain these many moons.

As the pirates advanced, one, with a quick eye, sighted Nibs disappearing through the woods.

"Shall I after him, Captain?" the pirate asked.

"Not now," Hook said darkly. "He is only one and I want to catch all seven. Scatter and look for them."

The men were a villainous-looking lot. In the midst of them, blackest and largest of them all, James Hook lay at his ease in a rough chariot drawn by his men. Instead of a right hand he had the iron hook with which he encouraged them to increase their pace. He was thin and black-visaged, with his hair hanging in long curls which gave him a sinister look. In his mouth he had a holder which enabled him to smoke two cigars at once. But undoubtedly the grimmest part of him was his

iron claw. Such was the terrible man against whom Peter Pan was pitted.

Now, as his men fanned out to look for the boys, he seemed moved to talk confidingly with his faithful bosun, Smee.

"Most of all," Hook was saying, "I want their captain, Peter Pan. 'Twas he cut off my arm." He brandished the hook threateningly. "I've waited long to shake his hand with this. Oh, I'll tear him!"

He cast a look of pride upon his iron hand and one of scorn upon the other. Then again he frowned.

"Peter flung my arm," he said, wincing, "to a crocodile that happened to be passing by."

"I have often," said Smee, "noticed your strange dread of crocodiles."

"Not of crocodiles," Hook corrected him, "but of that one crocodile." He lowered his voice. "It liked my arm so much, Smee, that it has followed me ever since, from sea to sea and from land to land, licking its lips for the rest of me."

"In a way," said Smee, "it's a sort of compliment."

"I want no such compliments," Hook barked angrily. "I want Peter Pan, who first gave the brute its taste for me."

He sat down on a large mushroom, and now there was a quiver in his voice. "Smee," he said huskily, "that crocodile would have had me before this, but by a lucky chance it swallowed a clock which goes *tick, tick* inside it, and so before it can reach me I hear the tick and bolt." He laughed, but in a hollow way.

"Some day," said Smee, "the clock will run down, and then he'll get you."

Hook wetted his dry lips. "Ay," he said, "that's the fear that haunts me."

Since sitting down he had felt curiously warm. "Smee," he said, "this seat is hot." He jumped up. He and Smee examined the huge mushroom on which he had been sitting. They tried to pull it up, and it came away at once in their hands, for it had no root. Stranger still, smoke

began at once to come up. The pirates looked at each other. "A chimney!" they both exclaimed.

They had indeed discovered the chimney of the home under the ground. Not only smoke came out of it; there came also children's voices. For so safe did the boys feel in their hiding place that they were gaily chattering. The pirates listened grimly, and then replaced the mushroom. They looked around them and noted the holes in the seven trees.

"Did you hear them say Peter Pan's away from home?" Smee whispered, fidgeting with his cutlass.

Hook stood for a long time lost in thought, and at last a curdling smile lit up his swarthy face. Smee had been waiting for it. "Unrip your plan, Captain," he cried eagerly.

"To return to the ship," Hook replied slowly through his teeth, "and cook a large rich cake of a jolly thickness with green sugar on it. We will leave the cake where the boys will find it. They will gobble it up because, having no mother, they don't know how dangerous 'tis to eat rich damp cake." He burst into laughter. "Aha, they will die!"

Smee had listened with growing admiration.

"It's the wickedest, prettiest policy ever I heard of," he cried; and in their exultation the two danced and sang:

> *Avast, belay, when I appear,*
> *By fear they're overtook;*
> *Nought's left upon your bones when you*
> *Have shaken claws with Hook.*

They began the chorus, but they never finished it, for another sound broke in and stilled them. It was at first a tiny sound, but as it came nearer it was more distinct.

Tick tick tick tick.

Hook stopped dancing, one foot in the air. He shuddered. "The crocodile," he gasped, and bounded away, followed by his bosun.

Now the boys came out once more into the open. Presently Nibs rushed breathless into their midst.

"I have seen a wonderful thing," he cried, as they gathered around him eagerly. "A great white bird. It is flying this way."

"What kind of a bird, do you think?"

"I don't know," Nibs said, "but it looks so weary, and as it flies it moans, 'poor Wendy.'"

Wendy was now almost overhead, and they could hear her plaintive cry. But more distinct came the shrill voice of Tinker Bell. The jealous fairy had now cast off all disguise of friendship, and was darting at her victim from every direction, pinching savagely.

"Hullo, Tink," cried the wondering boys.

Tink's reply rang out: "Peter wants you to shoot the Wendy."

It was not in their nature to question when Peter ordered.

Tootles had a bow and arrow with him, and Tink noted it. "Quick, Tootles, quick," she screamed. "Peter will be so pleased."

Tootles excitedly fitted the arrow to his bow. "Out of the way, Tink," he shouted. Then he fired, and Wendy fluttered to the ground with an arrow in her breast.

5. The Little House

"I have shot the Wendy," Tootles cried proudly to the other boys. "Peter will be so pleased with me."

Overhead Tinker Bell laughed, and went into hiding. The others did not hear her. They had crowded around Wendy, and as they looked a terrible silence fell upon the wood.

Slightly was the first to speak. "This is no bird," he said in a scared voice. "I think it must be a lady."

"A lady?" said Tootles, trembling.

"Now I see," Curly said; "Peter was bringing us a lady to take care of us at last, and you have killed her."

Tootles' face was very white. "I must go away," he said, shaking. "I am so afraid of Peter."

It was at this tragic moment that they heard a sound which made the heart of every one of them rise in his mouth. They heard Peter crow.

"Peter!" they cried, for it was always thus that he signaled his return.

"Hide her," they whispered, and gathered hastily around Wendy. But Tootles stood aloof. Again came that ringing crow, and Peter dropped down in front of them.

"Great news, boys," he cried. "I have brought at last a mother for you all. Have you not seen her? She flew this way."

"Peter," said Tootles quietly, "I will show her to you." To the others he said, "Stand back, let Peter see."

So they all stood back, and Peter looked at Wendy. Then he saw the arrow. He took it from her heart and faced his band.

"Whose arrow?" he demanded sternly.

"Mine, Peter," said Tootles, on his knees. Peter raised the arrow to use it as a dagger. Tootles did not flinch. "Strike, Peter," he said.

"I cannot strike," said Peter, with awe. "There is something stays my hand."

"It is she," cried Nibs, "the Wendy lady. See, she has raised her arm."

"She lives!" Peter said briefly. Then he knelt beside her and found his button, which she had put on the chain she wore around her neck. "See," he said, "the arrow struck against this. It is the kiss I gave her. It has saved her life."

"Listen to Tink," said Curly; "she is crying because the Wendy lives."

Then they had to tell Peter of Tink's crime, and almost never had they seen him look so stern.

"Listen, Tinker Bell," he cried, "I am your friend no more. Begone from me for ever." She flew on his shoulder and pleaded, but he brushed her off. Not until Wendy again raised her arm did he relent sufficiently to say, "Well, not for ever, but for a whole week."

But what to do with Wendy in her present delicate state of health?

"Let us carry her down into the house," Curly suggested.

"No, no," Peter said, "you must not touch her. It would not be sufficiently respectful."

"But if she lies there," Tootles said, "she will die."

"Ay," Slightly admitted, "but there is no way out."

"Yes, there is," cried Peter. "Let us build a little house around her."

They were all delighted. "Quick," he ordered them, "bring me, each of you, the best of what we have." In a moment they were scurrying this way and that, down for bedding, up for firewood; and while they were at it, who should appear but John and Michael. Peter had quite forgotten them.

"Curly," said Peter in his most captainy voice, "see that these boys help in the building of the house."

In the meantime the woods had been alive with the sound of axes; almost everything needed for a cosy dwelling already lay at Wendy's feet.

"If only we knew the kind of house she likes best," said one of the boys.

"Peter," shouted another, "she is moving in her sleep. Her mouth opens."

"Perhaps she is going to sing in her sleep," said Peter. "Wendy, sing the kind of house you would like to have."

Immediately, without opening her eyes, Wendy began to sing:

I wish I had a pretty house,
The littlest ever seen,
With funny little red walls,
And roof of mossy green.

By the greatest good luck the branches they had brought were sticky with red sap, and all the ground was carpeted with moss.

When the house was made just as Wendy had asked, Peter strode up and down ordering finishing touches. When it seemed absolutely finished, nothing remained to do but to knock.

The boys stood before the door, trying to look their best. Peter knocked politely.

The door opened, and a lady came out. It was Wendy. They all whipped off their hats.

Slightly was the first to speak. "Wendy lady," he said, "for you we built this house."

"Oh, say you're pleased," cried Nibs.

"Lovely, darling house," Wendy said, and they were the very words the boys had hoped she would say.

Then they all went on their knees and, holding out their arms, cried, "O Wendy lady, be our mother."

"Ought I?" Wendy said, all shining. "Of course, I am only a little girl, and I have no real experience."

And then, when they pleaded with her, "Very well," she said, "I

will do my best. Come inside at once, you naughty children; I am sure your feet are damp. And before I put you to bed I have just time to finish the story of Cinderella."

By and by she tucked them up in the great bed in the home under the trees, but she herself slept that night in the little house, and Peter kept watch outside with drawn sword, for the pirates could be heard carousing far away and the wolves were on the prowl.

6. The Home Under the Ground

How they grew to love their home under the ground; especially Wendy! It consisted of one large room with a floor in which you could dig, and in this floor grew stout mushrooms which were used as stools. A Never tree tried hard to grow in the center of the room, but every morning the boys sawed the trunk through, level with the floor. By evening it was always about two feet high, and then they put a board on top of it, the whole thus becoming a table. As soon as the meal was cleared away they sawed off the trunk again, and thus there was more room to play. There was an enormous fireplace, and across this Wendy stretched strings from which she suspended her washing. The bed was tilted against the wall by day, and let down at 6:30, when it filled nearly half the room, and all the boys except Michael slept in it. Wendy must have a baby, so Michael, being the littlest, was hung up in a basket.

There was one recess in the wall, no larger than a bird cage, which was the private apartment of Tinker Bell. It could be shut off from the rest of the home by a tiny curtain.

It was all especially entrancing to Wendy because those rampageous boys of hers gave her so much to do. The cooking kept her nose to the pot, and there were whole weeks when she was never above ground except on an occasional evening when she did her mending. Wendy's favorite time for sewing and darning was after the boys had all gone to bed.

As time wore on, did Wendy think much about the beloved parents she had left behind her? Perhaps; but she did not really worry about them. She was sure they would always keep the window open for her to fly back. What did disturb her at times was that John remembered his parents only vaguely, as people he had once known, and Michael was quite willing to believe that she was really his mother. These things scared her a little, and she tried to keep them remembering the old life.

When Peter was home he would help Wendy manage the children. But he never was really happy about pretending to be their father. Once he asked, anxiously, "It is only make-believe, isn't it? It would make me seem so old to be their father. I'm not really, Wendy?"

"Not if you don't wish it," Wendy answered him. Then she asked firmly, "Peter, what are your exact feelings toward me?"

"Those of a devoted son, Wendy."

"I thought so," she said, and went and sat by herself at the extreme end of the room.

"You are so queer," said Peter, puzzled.

Then came the evening which, though none of them knew it, was to be the last in their underground home. The day had been almost uneventful, and now the children were having their evening meal.

Above, the Indians were on guard. Tiger Lily, their beautiful princess, had once been saved by Peter from a dreadful fate at the hands of the pirates. Ever since, there was nothing she and her braves would not do for him. All night they would sit keeping watch over the home underground, awaiting the attack by the pirates that was sure to come.

The children were playing noisily when Wendy heard Peter's step above.

"Children, I hear your father's step," she said. "He likes you to meet him at the door."

Now they heard the Indians greet Peter. "Watch well, braves," Peter said as he passed them and began his descent through the tree.

Then, as so often before, the gay children rushed to drag Peter in. As so often before, but never again!

Now it was time for Wendy's good-night story, the story they loved best; the story Peter hated. Usually when she began to tell this story he left the room; but tonight he remained on his stool.

7. Wendy's Story

"Listen, then," said Wendy, settling down to her story, with Michael at her feet and seven boys in the bed. "There was once a gentleman——"

"I had rather he had been a lady," Curly said.

"Quiet," their mother scolded. "There was a lady also. The gentleman's name was Mr. Darling, and her name was Mrs. Darling."

"I knew them," John said, to annoy the others.

"I think I knew them," Michael said rather doubtfully.

"They were married," Wendy went on, "and what do you think they had?"

"White rats," cried Nibs, inspired.

"No! They had three children," said Wendy. "Now these three children had a faithful nurse called Nana; but Mr. Darling was angry with her and chained her up in the yard. And so all the children flew away.

They flew away to the Neverland, where the lost children are."

"Oh, Wendy," cried Tootles, "was one of the lost children called Tootles?"

"Hush! Now I want you to consider the feelings of the unhappy parents with all their children flown away. Think of the empty beds!"

"I don't see how it can have a happy ending," said the second twin.

"Have no fear," said Wendy. She had now come to the part that Peter hated. "You see," she went on, "the children knew that the mother would always leave the window open for them to fly back by; so they stayed away for years and had a lovely time. And when they were quite grown up they went back, and there was the window still standing open. So up they flew to their mummy and daddy, and pen cannot describe the happy scene."

When Wendy finished Peter uttered a hollow groan.

"What is it, Peter?" she cried, running to him.

"Wendy, you are wrong about mothers." And now he told what he had hitherto concealed.

"Long ago," he said, "I thought like you that my mother would always keep the window open for me, so I stayed away for moons and moons and moons, and then flew back; but the window was barred, and there was another little boy sleeping in my bed."

"Wendy, let us go home," cried John and Michael together.

"Yes," she said, clutching them.

"Not tonight?" asked the lost boys, bewildered.

"At once," said Wendy resolutely. "Peter, will you make the necessary arrangements?"

"If you wish it," he replied coolly. If she did not mind parting, he was going to show her that neither did he! But of course, he cared very much, and was full of wrath against grownups, who, as usual, were spoiling everything.

"Tinker Bell will take you across the sea," he said in a short sharp voice. "Wake her, Nibs."

Now Wendy saw that the boys were gazing very forlornly at her, and her heart melted.

"Dear ones," she said, "if you will all come home with me I feel almost sure I can get my father and mother to adopt you."

The boys jumped for joy. "Peter, can we go?" they all cried.

"All right," Peter replied with a bitter smile; and immediately they rushed to get their things.

"And now, Peter," Wendy said, thinking she had put everything right, "I am going to give you your medicine before you go." But then she saw a look on Peter's face that made her heart sink.

"I am not going with you, Wendy," he said.

"To find your mother," she coaxed.

"No!" he told Wendy. "Perhaps she would say I was old, and I just want always to be a little boy and to have fun."

And so the others had to be told. "Peter isn't coming."

Peter not coming! They gazed blankly at him, their sticks over their backs, and on each stick a bundle.

"Now then," cried Peter, "no fuss, no blubbering. Good-by, Wendy," and he held out his hand cheerily. She had to take his hand, as there was no indication that he would prefer a thimble.

"You will remember to take your medicine, Peter?"

"Yes."

That seemed to be everything, and an awkward pause followed. Peter, however, was not the kind that breaks down before people. "Are you ready, Tinker Bell?" he called out.

"Ay, ay."

"Then lead the way."

Tink darted up the nearest tree, but no one followed her, for it was at this moment that the pirates made their dreadful attack upon the Indians. Above, where all had been so still, the air was rent with shrieks and the clash of steel. Below, there was dead silence. Peter seized his sword, and the lust of battle was in his eye.

44

8. The Children Are Carried Off

The pirate attack had taken the Indians by surprise. Around the brave Tiger Lily were a dozen of her stoutest warriors. Suddenly without warning, they saw the pirates bearing down on them, and they seized their weapons. The air was torn with the war cry. But it was too late. Many were slain, and only Tiger Lily and a small remnant of her tribe escaped through the dark woods.

But for the victorious Hook the night's work was not yet over. It was not the Indians he had come to destroy. It was Peter Pan he wanted, Peter and Wendy and their band, but chiefly Peter.

In the meantime, the boys waited below to know their fate. Which side had won? The pirates, listening at the mouths of the trees, heard this question put by every boy, and, alas, they also heard Peter's answer.

"If the Indians have won," he said, "they will beat the tom-tom. It is always their sign of victory."

Now, Smee had found the tom-tom, and was at that moment sitting on it. To his amazement Hook signed to him to beat the tom-tom, and slowly there came to Smee an understanding of the dreadful wickedness of the order. Twice Smee beat upon the instrument, and then stopped to listen.

"The tom-tom," the pirates heard Peter cry. "An Indian victory!"

The children answered with a cheer that was music to the black hearts above. They repeated their good-bys to Peter. Rapidly and silently Hook gave his orders: one man to each tree, and the others to arrange themselves in a line two yards apart.

The first to emerge from his tree was Curly. He rose out of it into

the arms of one of the pirates, who flung him to another, and then to another, and so he was tossed from one to another until he fell at the feet of the black pirate. All of the boys were plucked and tossed in this ruthless manner, like bales of goods flung from hand to hand.

A different treatment was accorded to Wendy, who came last. With ironical politeness Hook raised his hat to her and, offering her his arm, escorted her to the spot where the others were being gagged and tied to prevent their flying away.

Hook now signed to his men that the captives were to be taken to the ship. The little house was to be used as a conveyance. The children were flung into it, four stout pirates raised it on their shoulders, the others fell in behind, and singing the hateful pirate chorus the strange procession set off through the woods.

Now Hook was alone. He tiptoed to one of the trees. Intently he listened for any sound from below. Was Peter asleep? Or did he stand waiting at the foot of the tree, with his dagger in his hand?

There was no way of knowing save by going down. Hook was a brave man; but for a moment he had to stop and wipe his brow, which was dripping like a candle. Then silently he let himself go down into the unknown.

He arrived at the foot of the shaft, and as his eyes became accustomed to the dim light, the only thing on which his greedy gaze rested —long sought for and found at last—was the great bed. On the bed lay Peter fast asleep.

Unaware of the tragedy being enacted above, Peter had, after the children left, played gaily on his pipes to prove to himself that he did not care. Then he decided not to take his medicine, so as to grieve Wendy. Then he lay down on the bed. He nearly cried; but it struck him how indignant Wendy would be if he laughed instead; so he laughed a haughty laugh, and fell asleep in the middle of it.

Thus defenseless, Hook found him. He stood silent at the foot of the tree, looking through a small opening. There across the chamber was his enemy. He made a stealthy step but found the way blocked by

a low door in the tree. Feeling for the catch, he found to his fury that it was beyond his reach. Was his enemy to escape him after all?

But what was that? The red in his eye had caught sight of Peter's medicine standing on a ledge within easy reach. Immediately he knew that the sleeper was in his power.

Lest he be taken alive, Hook always carried about his person a dreadful poison, blended by himself. Five drops of this he now added

to Peter's medicine. Then one long gloating look he cast upon his victim and, turning, wormed his way up the tree. Now, muttering strangely to himself, he stole away through the woods.

Peter slept on. It must have been not less than ten o'clock by the crocodile when he suddenly sat up in his bed, awakened by a soft tapping on the door of his tree. Peter felt for his dagger till his hand gripped it. Then he spoke. "Who is that?"

"Let me in, Peter."

It was Tink, and quickly he unbarred the door. She flew in excitedly, her face flushed and her dress stained with mud.

"What is it? Out with it!" Peter shouted; and she told him about the capture of Wendy and the boys.

Wendy bound, and on the pirate ship! "I'll rescue her," Peter cried, leaping at his weapons. He thought of something he could do to please her. He would take his medicine.

His hand closed on the fatal draught.

"No!" shrieked Tinker Bell, who had heard Hook muttering about his deed as he sped through the forest. "It is poisoned!"

"Poisoned? Who could have poisoned it?" Peter asked.

"Hook," replied Tinker Bell.

"Don't be silly. How could Hook have got down here? Besides, I never fell asleep." And Peter really believed this.

He raised the cup. Tink knew there was no time for words now; it was time for deeds. With one of her lightning movements she got between Peter's lips and the draught and drained it to the dregs.

"It was poisoned, Peter," she told him softly, "and now I am going to die."

"Oh Tink, did you drink it to save me?"

"Yes."

Already she was reeling in the air. Her wings could hardly carry her now. She lighted on Peter's shoulder and gave his chin a loving bite. Then, tottering to her chamber, she lay down on the bed.

Peter knelt beside her in distress. Every moment her light was growing fainter, and he knew that if it went out she would be no more. Her voice was so low that at first he could not make out what she said. Then he made it out. She was saying that she thought she could get well again if children believed in fairies.

Peter flung out his arms. There were no children there, and it was nighttime. But he called to all the boys and girls who might be dreaming of the Neverland: "Do you believe?" he cried.

Tink sat up in bed to listen to her fate.

"If you believe," Peter shouted to them, "clap your hands. Don't let Tink die."

Many clapped. Then the clapping stopped suddenly as if countless mothers had rushed to their nurseries to see what on earth was happening. But already Tink was saved. First her voice grew strong; then she popped out of bed and was flashing through the room.

"And now to rescue Wendy," said Peter.

The moon was riding in a cloudy heaven when Peter rose from his tree, his weapons strapped to his side, to set out upon his perilous quest. As he pressed through the silent forest he swore this terrible oath: "Hook or me this time!"

9. The Pirate Ship

One green light squinting over Kidd's Creek, near the mouth of the pirate river, marked where the brig, the *Jolly Roger,* lay low in the water. A few of the pirates leaned over the bulwarks, others sprawled about the deck.

Hook trod the deck in thought. It was his hour of triumph. Peter had been removed forever from his path — so he thought — and all the other boys were on the brig, about to walk the plank.

"Are all the children chained, so that they cannot fly away?" he shouted.

"Ay, ay," his men answered him.

"Then hoist them up."

The wretched prisoners were dragged from the hold, all except Wendy, and ranged in line in front of him.

"Now then, bullies," he said briskly, "six of you walk the plank tonight, but I have room for two cabin boys. Which of you is it to be?"

When all of the boys refused, Hook roared out, "That seals your doom. Bring up their mother. Get the plank ready."

They were only boys, and they went white as they saw two of the pirates preparing the fatal plank. But they tried to look brave when Wendy was brought up.

"Tie her up," Hook shouted.

He took a step toward Wendy. His intention was to turn her face so that she would see the boys walking the plank one by one. But he never reached her, never heard the cry of anguish he had hoped to wring from her. He heard something else instead. It was the terrible *tick-tick* of the crocodile.

They all heard it, and immediately every head was turned toward Hook. Very frightful it was to see the change that came over him. It was as if he had been clipped at every joint. He fell in a little heap.

"Hide me," he cried hoarsely.

The pirates gathered round him, all eyes averted from the Thing that was coming aboard. They had no thought of fighting it. It was Fate.

Only when Hook was hidden from them did the boys rush to the ship's side to see the crocodile climbing it. Then they got the strangest surprise of this Night of Nights, for it was no crocodile that was coming to their aid. It was Peter!

He signed to them not to give vent to any cry that might arouse suspicion. Then he went on ticking.

10. "Hook Or Me This Time"

Now Peter, his dagger in his hand, scaled the side of the brig as noiseless as a mouse. He was amazed to see the pirates cowering from him, with Hook in their midst as if he had heard the crocodile. "How clever of me," he thought.

It was at this moment that the quartermaster emerged from the forecastle and came along the deck. Peter struck true and deep. John clapped his hands on the ill-fated pirate's mouth to stifle the dying groan. The man fell forward, and four boys caught him to prevent the

thud. Then Peter gave the signal, and the body was cast overboard. There was a splash, and then silence.

None too soon Peter, every inch of him on tiptoe, vanished into the cabin; for more than one private was screwing up his courage to look around.

"It's gone, Captain," Smee said. "All's still again."

Slowly Hook let his head emerge from his ruff, and listened intently. There was not a sound, and he drew himself up firmly to his full height. "Then here's to Johnny Plank," he cried, hating the boys more than ever because they had seen him unbend. "Fetch the cat, Jukes. It's in the cabin."

The cabin! Peter was in the cabin. The children gazed at one another.

"Ay, ay," said Jukes blithely, and he strode into the cabin. They followed him with their eyes, while Hook began to sing:

> *Yo ho, yo ho, the scratching cat,*
> *Its tails are nine, you know,*
> *And when they're writ upon your back—*

What was the last line will never be known, for suddenly the song was stayed by a dreadful screech from the cabin. Then there was a crowing sound which was well understood by the boys, but to the pirates was almost worse than the screech.

"What was that?" cried Hook. The pirate named Cecco hesitated for a moment and then swung into the cabin. At once he tottered out, haggard.

"What's the matter with Bill Jukes, you dog?" hissed Hook.

"The matter with him is he's dead, stabbed," replied Cecco in a hollow voice. "The cabin's black as a pit, but there's something terrible in there—the thing you heard crowing."

"Cecco," said Hook, in his most steely voice, "go back and fetch me out that doodle-doo."

Cecco, bravest of the brave, cowered before his captain, crying,

"No, no!" But Hook was purring to his claw.

"Did you say you would go, Cecco?" he said. Cecco went. There was no more singing, all listened now. And again came a death-screech and again a crow.

"'Sdeath and odds fish," thundered Hook, "who is to bring me that doodle-doo?" But none of the crew would go.

Seizing a lantern and raising his claw with a menacing gesture, Hook shouted, "I'll bring out that doodle-doo myself," and he sped into the cabin. In a moment he came staggering out, without his lantern.

"Something blew out the light," he said unsteadily.

"What of Cecco?" demanded a pirate named Noodler.

"He's as dead as Jukes," said Hook shortly.

One after another the men took up the cry, "The ship's doomed." At this the children could not resist raising a cheer. Hook had forgotten his prisoners, but now his face lit up again.

"Lads," he cried to his crew, "open the cabin door and drive them in. Let them fight the doodle-doo. If they kill him, we're that much better off. If he kills them, we're none the worse."

For the last time his men admired Hook, and devotedly they did his bidding. The boys, pretending to struggle, were pushed into the cabin and the door was closed on them.

"Now, listen," cried Hook, and all listened. But not one dared to face the door. Yes, one: Wendy, who all this time had been bound to the mast. But it was for neither a scream nor a crow that she was waiting. It was for the reappearance of Peter.

She had not long to wait. In the cabin he had found the thing for which he had gone in search: the key that would free the children of their manacles. And now they all stole forth, armed with such weapons as they could find. First signing to them to hide, Peter cut Wendy's bonds, and then nothing could have been easier than for them all to fly off together. But one thing barred the way: Peter's oath, "Hook or me this time." So when he had freed Wendy he whispered to her to

conceal herself with the others, and himself took her place by the mast, her cloak around him so that he should pass for her. Then he took a great breath and crowed.

To the pirates it was a voice crying that all the boys lay slain in the cabin; and they were panic-stricken.

"Lads," cried Hook now, "I've thought it out. There's a Jonah aboard."

"Ay," they snarled, "a man with a hook."

"No, lads, no, it's the girl. Never was luck on a pirate ship with a woman aboard. Fling the girl overboard," cried Hook.

The men rushed at the figure in the cloak. "There's none can save you now, missy," they jeered.

"There's one," replied the figure.

"Who's that?"

"Peter Pan, the avenger!" came the terrible answer; and as he spoke Peter flung off his cloak. "Down, boys, and at them," Peter's voice rang out, and in another moment the clash of arms was resounding through the ship. Had the pirates kept together they might have won; but they were all unstrung, and ran hither and thither, each thinking himself the last survivor of the crew. Some of them leaped into the sea. Others hid in the dark, only to fall easy prey to the swords of the boys.

All were gone when a group of boys surrounded Hook, who seemed to have a charmed life. They had done for his men, but this man alone seemed to be a match for them all.

Suddenly another sprang into the fray.

"Put up your swords, boys," cried the newcomer, brandishing his sword in a commanding manner. "This man is mine."

Thus suddenly Hook found himself face to face with Peter. The others drew back and formed a ring around them.

"Proud and insolent youth," said Hook, "prepare to meet thy doom."

"Dark and sinister man," Peter answered, "have at thee."

Without more words they fell to and for a space there was no advantage to either. Peter was a superb swordsman, but his shorter reach stood him in ill stead. Yet, though Hook kept forcing him back, the pirate could not get the better of him. Suddenly the sword fell from Hook's hand, and he was at Peter's mercy.

"Now!" cried all the boys. But with a magnificent gesture Peter invited Hook to pick up his sword.

"Pan, who and what art thou?" Hook cried huskily.

"I'm youth, I'm joy," Peter answered, "I'm a little bird that has broken out of the egg."

This, of course, was nonsense; but it made Hook more unhappy than ever. He fought like a human flail, but Peter fluttered around him, and again and again he darted in and pricked.

Hook was fighting now without hope. Abandoning the fight, he rushed into the room where the gunpowder was stored, and fired it.

"In two minutes," he cried, "the ship will be blown to pieces." But Peter issued from the powder magazine with the shell in his hands, and calmly flung it overboard.

Seeing Peter slowly advancing upon him through the air with dagger poised, Hook sprang upon the bulwarks to cast himself into the sea. He did not know that the crocodile was waiting for him, for the clock inside the crocodile had stopped. As the black pirate stood on the bulwark looking over his shoulder, Peter glided through the air and pushed him off with his foot. Thus perished James Hook.

Then the boys took over the ship. A few sharp orders were given by Captain Pan, and they turned the ship around and nosed her for the mainland.

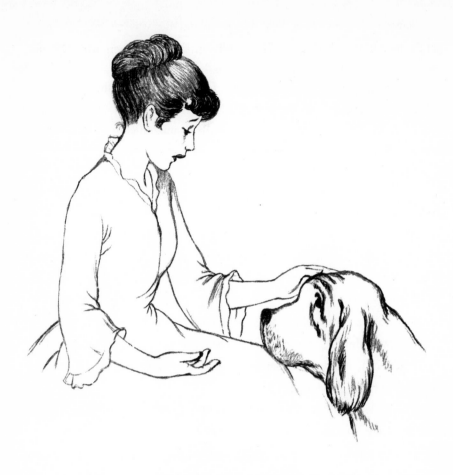

11. The Return Home

Meantime, what was happening in that desolate home from which the three children took such heartless flight so long ago?

On that eventful evening to which we have now come, Mrs. Darling was in the night-nursery awaiting her husband's return home. She had fallen asleep in her chair. Suddenly she started up, calling the children's names; but there was no one in the room but Nana.

"Oh Nana, I dreamt my dear ones had come back."

Nana had filmy eyes, but all she could do was to put her paw gently in her mistress's lap. They were sitting thus when Mr. Darling came home from the office. He was tired.

"Won't you play me to sleep on the nursery piano?" he asked. And as Mrs. Darling was crossing to the day-nursery he added thoughtlessly, "And shut that window. I feel a draught."

"Oh George, never ask me to do that. The window must be left open for them always, always."

He begged her pardon, and she went into the day-nursery and played, and soon Mr. Darling was asleep. While he slept, Peter flew into the room with Tinker Bell.

"Quick, Tink," he whispered, "close the window; bar it. That's right. Now you and I must get away by the door, and when Wendy comes she will think her mother has barred her out; and she will have to come back with me."

Then he peeped into the day-nursery to see who was playing. He whispered to Tink, "It's Wendy's mother."

He did not know the tune, which was "Home, Sweet Home," but he knew it was saying, "Come home, Wendy, Wendy, Wendy," and he cried, "You will never see Wendy again, lady, for the window is barred."

He peeped in again to see why the music had stopped; and now he saw that Mrs. Darling had laid her head on her arm, and that two tears were sitting on her eyes.

"She wants me to unbar the window," thought Peter. "She's awfully fond of Wendy." Then, after a pause, "I'm fond of her, too. We can't both have her, lady."

He ceased to look at her, but even then she would not let go of him. It was just as if she were inside him, knocking.

"Oh, all right," he said at last, and gulped. Then he unbarred the window. "Come on, Tink," he cried, "We don't want any silly mothers." And he flew away.

Thus Wendy and John and Michael found the window open for them after all. They alighted on the floor and looked about. It was then that Mrs. Darling began playing again.

"It's Mother!" cried Wendy, peeping.

"Let us creep in," John suggested, "and put our hands over her eyes." But Wendy, who saw that they must break the joyous news more gently, had a better plan.

Let us all slip into our beds and be there when she comes in, just as if we had never been away."

And so, when Mrs. Darling went back to the night-nursery to see if her husband was asleep, all the beds were occupied. The children waited for her cry of joy, but it did not come. She saw them, but then, she saw them in their beds so often in her dreams that she thought this was just the dream still. She sat down in the chair by the fire, where in the old days she had nursed them.

"Mother!" Wendy cried.

"That's Wendy," she said, but still she was sure it was the dream.

"Mother!"

"That's John," she said.

"Mother!" cried Michael. He knew her now.

"That's Michael," she said, and she stretched out her arms for the three children they would never envelop again. Yes, they did! They went around Wendy and John and Michael, who had slipped out of bed and run to her.

"George, George," she cried, when she could speak, and Mr. Darling woke to share her bliss, and Nana came rushing in. There could not have been a lovelier sight; but there was none to see it except a strange boy who was staring in at the window. He had ecstasies innumerable that other children can never know; but he was looking through the window at the one joy from which he must forever be barred.

The six boys had been waiting below to give Wendy time to ex-

plain about them. When they went up, Mrs. Darling said at once that she would have them, though Mr. Darling did think six a rather large number. Somehow, they were all fitted in.

As for Peter, he saw Wendy once again before he flew away. He did not exactly come to the window, but he brushed against it in passing, so that she could open it if she liked and call to him. That was what she did.

"Hullo, Wendy, good-by," he said.

"Oh dear, are you going away?" Wendy asked.

"Yes."

Mrs. Darling came to the window, for she was keeping a sharp eye on Wendy. She told Peter that she had adopted all the other boys and would like to adopt him also.

"No," said Peter. "I don't want to go to school and learn solemn things. I don't want to be a man. I want always to be a boy and have fun."

"But where are you going to live?" Mrs. Darling asked him.

"With Tink in the house we built for Wendy. The fairies are going to put it high up among the tree tops where they sleep at nights."

"It will be rather lonely in the evening," said Wendy.

Mrs. Darling saw his mouth twitch, and she made him this offer: she would let Wendy go to him for a week every year to do his spring cleaning. This promise sent Peter away quite gay again.

"You won't forget me, Peter will you?" Wendy called to him. Peter promised; and then he flew away.

and found herself lying on the bank, with her head in the lap of her sister, who was gently brushing away some dead leaves that had fluttered down from the trees upon her face.

"Wake up, Alice dear!" said her sister. "Why, what a long sleep you've had!"

"Oh, I've had such a curious dream!" said Alice. And she told her sister, as well as she could remember them, all these strange Adventures of hers that you have just been reading about; and, when she had finished, her sister kissed her, and said "It *was* a curious dream, dear, certainly; but now run in to your tea: it's getting late." So Alice got up and ran off, thinking while she ran, as well she might, what a wonderful dream it had been.